C000110931

'Skinheads were the demo
Respectable society steered clear. In this blistering
yet touching novel we see that world from the
inside, from someone who was there, the clothes
and the sounds, the hatred and the fights, but also
the camaraderie and the love. Not since *Brighton
Rock* has a south-coast town and its people been
portrayed so vividly and compellingly.'
Kester Aspden, author of The Hounding of David
Oluwale

Howard Cunnell was born in Eastbourne, East Sussex, and lives in London. He has worked as a scuba diving instructor, lifeguard, and labourer. He is the editor of Jack Kerouac's *On the Road – The Original Scroll*, and is a Leverhulme Research Fellow at the University of Sussex. *Marine Boy* is his first novel.

This book is published by
SOUL BAY PRESS LTD
SUSSEX

Soul Bay Press Limited
3rd Floor Map House
34-36 St Leonards Road
Eastbourne
East Sussex
BN21 3UT
Registered in England No: 06322122
Registered office as above

First Edition 2008

Set in Palatino Linotype 10pt

Cover by Alan Stepney & Daniel Conway
Typeset by DC & APF
Soul Bay Press Logo © Alan Stepney & Andy Franks
Printed and bound in United Kingdom by Anthony Rowe, CPI Group

A CIP catalogue for this book is available from the British Library
ISBN: 978-0-9559553-0-3

MARINE BOY

a novel

By

HOWARD CUNNELL

for Mark

It was today – rather yesterday I think – that he told me it was important not to accept life as a brutal approximation. I said people don't talk like that in this neighborhood.

Jim Harrison, Dalva

There was a lot of blood. The door from the close, hot bedroom to the front room was open now. Scott had cut the black cable ties that had held me to the little cot bed and he was kind of cradling me so that I could sit up. Through into the front room I could see curved sprays of blood like surf splashes up the walls, and a spreading pool of blood on the rough wood floor. The skin on my wrists had been rubbed away and was red and sore where the cable ties had dug in. There was one table lamp shaped like a greaser smoking a fat joint and riding a chopped Harley to nowhere, the dirty torn shade a Stars and Stripes. The lamp's beach fire orange light threw further shapes into the room, and the amplified shadow of the stoned ceramic biker loomed high up on the wall. I was on the little cot bed with Scott's black Harrington jacket over me and I was kind of shaking and hugging myself the way you see crazy people do. Scott held me tighter and I could hear him breathing in and out like a fighting dog at rest. There was nothing else I could see in the front room that wasn't broken.

Eddie Beer looked like he'd been swimming hard in blood for a long time and was ready to give up and drown. His hands and bitten down fingers were red. The steel toecaps showing through the torn away leather of his boots were wet and shiny. You couldn't see the home-made swastika and lightning bolt tattoos on his face for all the blood. He sat quiet and still like a beaten child, close by Bombhead with his back against the far wall, and he didn't move as the tide of blood started to rise and soak his jeans.

Now the action was over Bombhead wasn't doing anything. He was leaning dark and massive and silent against the wall with his left leg bent and the sole of one ten hole Doc Marten boot flat against the wall. His arms were folded and his eyes were half closed and he'd thumbed a smear of blood across his face like it was war paint and he looked like he was thinking about nothing at all. He could have been waiting for a bus into town. His white knife-edged Sta-Prest were stained here and there with red rosettes and pinky blooms.

11

Dawn was standing next to Eddie and she was stroking his shaved head and talking quietly to him. There were large bloody handprints on her bleached and skin-tight Levi's. I wanted to call out to her but I didn't. My mouth and throat were bruised and tasted sour. To tell you the honest truth I didn't trust myself to speak without crying and I had decided sometime in the days and nights before that I would try not to cry anymore. It had seemed then to be the only thing I could decide on. Nothing else had been up to me. Dawn was stroking Eddie Beer's scarred and bloody head and looking around the flat as if it had been decorated to try and please her. As though all the blood splashed up the walls and thickening on the floor was clean new paint covering at last the dirty, worn, and unpainted rooms of her too short and lonely childhood.

Bombhead moved to slowly reach down and pick up from the soaked floor by his boots a bloody trashed picture of Dawn in a cheap broken frame. The picture showed Dawn when she was little, proper little I mean, maybe eight or nine, and barefoot, and camping out with her Dad at a once a year bikers festival called the Bulldog Bash. She had long black hair layered and feathering out either side of a jagged centre part, and she was wearing greasy cut-offs and a dirty white T-shirt with a red star on it. She was holding a can of Breaker beer and firing off a v-sign. In the background you could see a lot of tents, some blown in and collapsed, and shining bikes and flared jeans and dirty boots and empty cans and mud all around. Dawn was smoking a cigarette and looking fierce.

Once, and what seemed to me to be a long time ago, she had shown me the picture and told me it was one of only two her Dad had ever taken of her. A little while after that, I can't remember when, I had bought and given her the little frame. Bombhead looked at the picture and he looked at Dawn with her vanilla yellow boot girl haircut growing out black at the roots. Bombhead held the picture out to her and she took it, blood and all. I knew she would want to have it where she was going. Bombhead and Dawn looked at each other and grinned.

"You haven't grown much," Bombhead said.

"Big enough to kick you in your half caste bollocks," she said, making to kick him.

"Oi," Scott said to them softly, his breathe warm on my face, "That's enough," and they stopped.

I could smell blood and petrol, the thick clinging Rocky hash Eddie Beer had started smoking, and a wet burning close by. Eddie was humming, it sounded like. Burnt black paper spiralled and fell in the room like wet autumn leaves. There were bloody drag marks going from all the blood on the floor towards the front door.

"Shouldn't we be getting out of here?" Bombhead said.

Scott and me looked at Bombhead and then we looked over at Al Babe.

Al Babe had his shirt off and was drying himself with a dirty beach towel. His sea green eyes were wide open and shining with what he had done and what he had seen. Al Babe ran deep. He believed, or he said he did, that the skinheads were the risen warriors of Aelle, the Anglo-Saxon chief who in a bloody massacre had sacked the castle at Pevensey Bay, then called Anderida, in 491 or so, and who after this victory over the Britons had established the Kingdom of Sussex. Al Babe believed that the sleeping ancient kingdom waited to be remade on the beaches and downs where we lived. The castle was a mile or two east from the broken and bloodstained rooms where we were now gathered in the dark. Al Babe meant to keep Sussex white and at times that summer I thought there would be trouble with Bombhead about that, but the boys had their heads tuned in to what Scott wanted and they managed to keep the peace.

Standing blond and tan and beautiful Al Babe looked lost to his dreams of revenge. There was blood on his boots and jeans. There was blood on all of them. Al Babe had no tattoos on his smooth and sun blushed skin. His golden crop had spots of blood in it.

When Al Babe saw me looking at him through the open door Scott, holding me with blood on his hands, said, "Al Babe, are you with us mate? Go and tell Gaz to bring the car in."

Al Babe shook himself and nodded and went out the door still bare-chested. He left the door to the yard open. Light came in from the full moon. I heard his boots ringing on the metal stairs that went down to the yard. A rolling salty breeze came in off the sea and sent more burned paper swirling in the room. Eddie slowly moved his head to look at it. The sea breeze backed up and the front door slammed shut and the burned paper fell slowly to the floor. After a little while Al Babe came back.

"Car's ready," he said.

"Put these jeans on Kim," Scott said.

He was holding a pair of clean sun faded Levi's with a button fly but I didn't take them. I was staring at Eddie Beer. He was tracing patterns in the thick wet blood on his jeans.

"Eddie," Scott called to him, "Eddie."

Eddie looked at Scott but I don't know if he saw him.

"Go somewhere and wash up," Scott said, "Get rid of them jeans."

"Fuck Scott," said Al Babe, "Look at him. He needs to get rid of everything. We all do."

"I'm not finished," Scott said. "Bomb?"

Bombhead said, "Take him to my house Al. My Nan won't say anything. Stay in the alleys and keep off Seaside Road. Get him in the bath. Give him some of my clothes and burn his."

Al Babe didn't like taking orders from Bombhead but he was a good soldier as well as a white man. And we all knew that Al Babe did what Bombhead said as much for Scott as for anything else. Al Babe loved Scott. We all did. Still it wasn't like Bombhead needed anybody to back him up, the size and the colour he was. He could beat you with his low sure voice too, the authority in it. He could make anybody jump right enough. Al Babe went over to Eddie and said something to him. Eddie got up and they went out together. I could see outlines of running horses finger drawn in blood on his jeans.

"I can have some of his clothes?" I heard Eddie say to Al Babe.

Dawn came tracking blood into the bedroom and helped me on with the Levi's. I was still shaking and my fingers wouldn't work and she buttoned the jeans for me and put her hand on my cropped down hair and stroked me. The sound was loud inside my head. She looked at me with her kohl-lined blazing green Pharaoh eyes that knew everything.

"He cut your hair," she said, "Oh Kim man he cut your hair."

Bombhead put his big hand on Dawn's head.

"Last train Dawn," he said, "Chop chop," and then to Scott he said, "We need to get out of here mate."

Scott said, "Take Kim down to the beach Bomb."

I looked into Scott's face, deeply tan and darker still in shadow, and Bombhead must have seen something in me when I looked at him.

"I think you should take him Scott," he said.

"I haven't finished here," Scott said.

"I'll do it. Take him mate," Bombhead said, "He's your blood."

Scott looked crazy at me for a minute and then he didn't. Whatever he was thinking when he looked at me passed across his face like a rain dark wind-blown cloud and was quickly gone. He looked at Bombhead and Bombhead nodded and then Scott looked at me again.

"Horse?" he said.

"You take me," I said.

To tell you the truth I didn't know who I was in any way that mattered. All I could see was too much blood. Blood splashed up the walls and all over the skinheads and soaking across the floor and stuck under Scott's fingernails. I was the only one bleeding. There was sticky leaking blood in my hair from a big cut on my head. There was dried blood in an older cut on my cheek where Scott had hit me. I didn't sound like me anymore and I guess I wasn't but I could still talk. I didn't cry. For some reason I couldn't think of anything worse than crying in front of Scott and the skinheads.

"I want you to take me Scott."

I held onto him tightly and Scott touched me gently like he was brushing the hair that wasn't there anymore from my eyes and carried me out into the late summer night. I'm a head taller than him and he carried me easily, or so it seemed to me then. I thought I could hear the sea but I don't know, it might have just been something I heard inside me. Bombhead followed us.

"Did you kill him?" I said.

Scott just carried me and shushed me.

Gary Angelino, blond, thirteen years old, monkey-faced, off his head, wearing a black Harrington and boots and tight white jeans, sat behind the wheel of a stolen Cresta pale under the moon and leaned over to open the door. He looked at me, his blue eyes big and wide.

"Shit," he said, "look at his face."

Scott put me in the back seat and I sat and watched as Bombhead doused the two chopped bikes in the yard with petrol. Dawn came out of the door of what had once been her home carrying a green jerry can of petrol. She stood in the black doorway and turned and threw the jerry can back into the room. I watched her dig inside her tight jeans until she found a book of matches. Dawn lit up the whole book and threw it inside the door. Bright orange fire flared in the black hole of the doorway. Dawn skipped down the metal stairs with fire at her back. Bombhead set fire to the bikes. There was a wumpfh and the fire caught and held. Dawn and Bombhead got in the back of the car with me. Scott sat in the front. We watched the flames until it got hot in the car. Scott barked a hard laugh and I was scared that everything was going to explode.

"Let's go," my brother said.

A YEAR or so ago, when I still believed that happiness could be found in following the summer all around, I sat on a hot and windswept Moroccan beach in early November with my brother Scott under what seemed to me to be the familiar peachy light of our boyhoods. He had said that he thought they were playing at being skinheads, most of them.

"But not her though Kim, you know how I felt about her."

And the thing, of course, was that I didn't. I had never known how Scott felt about Dawn. Since it happened I don't remember Scott and I ever talking about her. I don't really know how Scott feels about anything that happened that summer long ago when everything changed, or what he thinks when he remembers Bombhead and Al Babe and Gary Angelino, and because this was so I was ready to hear his side of any part of the story he wanted to tell me.

I mean I was sleeping with her, at least at the beginnning, but I can't tell you a lot about Dawn myself. At the finish she told me what she got out of being a skinhead. I didn't have the good sense to ask her at the start, and after that things got away from me and there never seemed to be a right time. There's a big difference between thinking about somebody the way I thought about Dawn and caring about them enough to help them. It's hard to look up from your own life. Plus she was tough. Some people give off a help me vibe but Dawn never did. So the way I thought about Dawn was all about me. Whether I'd get what I wanted from her. A chance to cut her and to get her to cut me. Some Rocky and a ride maybe.

I'd say now that Scott was right about her, Dawn wasn't playing. If I wanted to be clever I could say Scott's always right because he believes what he says and he thinks about it before he says it, but he was right.

Most of the skinheads were playing and so were the Persians the skinheads spent the summer fighting. Some of the skinheads like Al Babe were playing harder than others and some, like Bombhead and especially Dawn, Pharaoh eyed and monkey booted, all sharp elbows and hard knees and cunts and fuck yous, weren't playing at all. Scott too. I don't know everything about my brother even now, and couldn't tell you how he feels about a lot of things, but I know enough to know that Scott wasn't playing in those days.

Scott has big thick hands that seem to belong to somebody else and sometimes I think that my brother looks like he has been made and melted down from somebody bigger and his hands were left over. I'm a head taller than him but there seems to be more squeezed into him. He has a big wide nose like a bull terrier, and he has high cheeks that go brick red when he's drunk or ready to fight. He has gold shining eyes and an overbite that makes him look like he's always thinking about something he's not ready to tell you about. If he does ever tell you, if he has thought about something long enough to say that it is this way or that with him, you will never get him to change his mind.

People say we look alike but I don't know. He's fairer than me though we both have these full lips and this dog nose, and with the sun on us neither of us look English. My wife and her family joke with me about this and talk about me being a throwback. My eyes are brown and really dark. I'm clumsy though, except in the water, and I stand out. Scott's graceful and he can pretty much make himself invisible when he needs to. I talk too much and Scott, well he hardly says anything at all.

Sitting facing the Atlantic in Essaouira on the long beach that curved south under old fort walls, with my two youngest daughters darkening and sandy like the returned and happy ghosts of our younger selves, I wondered if deep down the long ago summer I'm going to tell you about was the last time Scott had felt certain about himself or about anything at all. His new three-

quarter length sleeve of red and saffron lotus flowers
and black grey rocks and falling water covered up some
of the old tattoos, the ones I knew he was ashamed of
though I never heard him say so. You would never get
Scott to admit to a lack of certainty. Coming up Scott
always seemed the most certain person I knew.

"I've got nothing to say sorry for," he said.

I think maybe Scott was just remembering when he
was young and strong and the world seemed made only
for him. We've all felt that way I guess. With the sun in
my eyes my daughters playing on the shoreline became
strong black shapes gold lighted at the edges like figures
in a dream you can't quite remember. The wind
whipped in their loose dark hair so that it looked like
ribbon sea grass moving in the tidal wash of shallow
water.

I think now that Scott saying he had nothing to be
sorry for was a big thing for him. You might not think so
but you don't know him. It meant he thought there
might be.

While I watched Jay and Suzy throw Scott's yellow
frisbee I waited for my brother to say something else. I
was used to waiting for him to talk but unless he's high
or you get him on to music or travelling Scott doesn't
say much. Jay tried to show Suzy how to wait for the
wind to drop before passing the frisbee but Suzy just
liked to throw the frisbee into the wind any old how and
watch the patterns it made. I could hear Suzy laughing
and Jay's voice rising in anger.

I caught a Berber girl staring at me. She was young
but she had stars tattooed on her forehead with soot and
laurel. The rest of her face was covered by her hijab. I
smiled at her. These days, I'm tattooed wall to wall with
mantras, blessings, and good luck charms meant to stop
me hurting myself and other people. They work when I
remember I have them, and it's mostly when little kids
see me, and smile and go crazy with how I look, that I
remember.

Scott looked out to sea in the way that I had watched

him look out when we were little. As though he were always seeing some other magic land out there beyond the bright shining water.

"What have you come out here to hear me say?" he said at last.

I looked at him. For years while he was travelling he had let his hair grow long until it locksed up but his head was shaved again now. He was still slight and boyish but he looked to me like an old jockey who has to sweat down before a race. His hard look and his tight body were telling me and everybody else that he was still in the game that maybe only he was playing, but if you looked closely you might say that he was only just hanging on. The bumps and lines and marks and small scars on his face were evidence of how bloody mindedly he had moved through the world for over forty years. Always on his own terms. From the day he walked out of prison never doing anything he didn't want to do. All our lives I was supposed to be the clever one, though I'm not so sure it's ever done me any good, but I was clever enough to know that there wasn't a good answer to Scott's question.

I looked at his blue body board next to him on the sand. You might think the board was something a kid or a younger man might use, but surfing was Scott's thing now, and of course he was good at it. Made no difference to him how old he was. If Scott wanted to surf he was going to surf. That was what he was in Morocco for. Me, I love to dive and for a time I earned my money that way, in places like the Red Sea and thereabouts. It's all the same thing. We come from the sea, my brother and me, and when we are in the water we are home in a way that my wife, for one, finds difficult to understand.

"I don't know," I said, although I did. "I'm just having a hard time getting past it. It comes and goes, but I'm not doing that well with it just now."

"Mate," he said, "you're here, the kids are here, and you've got a great set-up at home, so why do you keep going over it?"

Scott sat with his big hands open in his lap and he looked down at them, at the lines that tracked and crossed so deeply there as if he were asking, these lines were not here before, how did they get here?

The thick quiet that fell between us again was like something you could reach out and touch. There was sand and grit in the air all around. I believed I would never hear what I wanted him to say. Scott is hard, that's as plain as day, and that hardness is at the heart of any story I can tell about my brother and me. Scott is hard in the way so many boys without fathers are hard, because he's had to be, and part of that hardness is never saying sorry and never asking for help or forgiveness. Scott would say look, I just don't talk when I don't have anything to say. When he's high you can't get him to shut up, but he's no different to anybody else I know with that. All the not talking though, that's part of the hard mask Scott picked up and put on a long time ago.

I didn't have to be hard because Scott was and I've never really stopped blaming him for that when all along I should have been thanking him. I would have liked to really talk about it but part of Scott's hardness, like not saying sorry, is not talking about things you feel. Talking that way is not done I guess. Scott's never asked me what happened in that place in the time before he came for me or what it has cost me in the years afterwards. I know now, at last, that it's not what you say that matters but what you do, and what's in your heart when you're doing it. Scott did come for me and take me out of there all those years ago, and because he did my honey-coloured daughters were walking up the gently canted beach to us with the sun and the spangled water behind them, and they were shouting "Dad! Daddy! Uncle Scott!"

"It was twenty years ago," he said, "and you're still trying to figure it out."

"Everything else seems to come from it though, don't you think?"

"Only if you let it," he said.

"Maybe so."

"He's dead. He's been dead a long time."

"Yes," I said.

"Now who's not talking?" my brother said.

Scott's right, it was a long time ago. Persia is not called Persia anymore, and I don't know where Dawn has gone. A lot of the other boys are lost and gone forever, and Scott? Scott can't stay in one place for very long. I can't help but think that's because he had to sit in prison for more than two years when he was bursting for life and ever since he's been trying to catch up, or maybe just go back in his heart to a time before he was locked up and forget it ever happened. And just maybe he's been running away from how he felt about what happened to me. And of course this was what I thought I always wanted him to say and didn't think I ever would.

Sometimes at home and late at night I'll pick a book off the shelf that I haven't read for a while and when I open it an old postcard from Scott will fall out from between the pages where I put it for safe-keeping or as a marker long ago. I'm passing the time, and it's likely I'll be high and waiting for my wife to come home, but when these cards fall and I pick them from the floor and read them I am with Scott in all the high hot countries. He loves the beach for sure but Scott also loves to get up in the mountains, above the clouds and far away.

One night when she had come back and found me sitting in the near dark, high and drinking vodka and reading some of Scott's old postcards from, I think, Pakistan, my wife said, "What happens when the road runs out? Scott never goes back to the places he's been before. What happens when the road runs out and he hasn't found what he's looking for? Where will he go then?"

She turned another lamp on in the room. She was speaking about Scott but she was talking to me. There is an American poet my wife likes. What I stand for, he said, is what I stand on, but I've heard that before, and my dive bag is always packed for the next trip out. The dream of wearing shorts forever my wife says, from another poem. She says I'm angry because Scott got away and I'm still locked into what happened. I don't know that Scott did get away to be honest, but she's right about me being angry with him.

This story is then maybe not about me, or the white school on the downs that I was sent to and what happened to me there before any of this, or about me and Dawn and her crazy, crazy Dad and the skinheads and the Persians, but about me and Scott, still like two hungry dogs locked in a small room and looking for a way out after all this time and all these years. But then I don't know. When you start you never know what part of a story will be the part where the light comes in, the part that speaks to you, and that you won't be able to forget.

YOU HAVE to start somewhere and so I'll say that I was sixteen and it was summer and I was back from the special school on the Sussex downs they had sent me to the winter before. Up in my high room, when the nights began to warm as early summer came, I used to dream about being back on the beach, but when I got home in that first week of June I went straight out to find Dawn rather than swim. That's what she was to me in those days.

I came home on the train, walking from the white school to the railway station down a sun-halved hill that was covered in cowslips, the bottoms of my Lee jeans grassy and dewy wet. Grasshoppers popped around my boots. I sat on the train watching the country go by, the green sea of the downs rising beyond the farms and small towns. Dirty sheep littered the fields like torn pages from a newspaper.

I put my bag in my room and I pulled on an old pair of cut-offs and flip-flops and went back out into the narrow hall that was warmed and lit by the sun through the open door. There was nobody home. Mum and Scott were at work. Mum cleaning some other family's house and Scott roofing. I went into the small, cool kitchen and ate a handful of dry Sugar Puffs and opened the fridge and took out a bottle of cold milk and drank some. Through the kitchen window I could see Mum's faded blue sunbed in the small back garden. I went back out into the hall wiping milk from my chin and then went out through the door and into wide open golden southern sunlight. The air was sweet and salt tasting. The water was sun lighted and low but beginning to rise up the beach in shallow and gently rolling terraced breakers. I promised myself I'd swim after I'd seen Dawn. I couldn't see any end to the beach or to the water and I believed it would always be there for me. We are each of us our own brightest star.

I walked west along the beach in the bright shining light of the day until I came to the Pier and then I turned inland and went into town to look for her. I knew where she would be and she was. She was drinking a can of Breaker in The Painted Wagon. She was fourteen then, I think. Her green eyes were lined with kohl so that she looked like a boy Pharaoh. I could smell vanilla on her. She'd put it in her hair. It was dark in the Wagon as the summer morning turned to afternoon, and we were up and away from the beaches and the incoming sunlit tide. We couldn't hear the noise of the breaking surf or see the high open sky or watch the honeyed southern light falling slowly all around.

All right, I'll tell you the truth, seeing Dawn with her black hair bleached blonde and cropped down so short did surprise me. I thought that I knew her even though I hadn't seen her for a term. I think now a term was too long. When you're young just one day can last forever. I had asked her to send pictures to the school but it turned out the pictures she sent me were from before, when she still had her black Mohawk. She had never written anything to me about changing into a skinhead while I was in there. So all the come on Polaroids she sent me, the little pictures of her wearing bondage combat trousers and sticking her black spiked hair up and her tongue out; I thought that was what she still looked like.

Before I went away there were a few punks left, and Taylor and Ted Beaumont and Donnie Orange had the Rebel thing going: flat tops from Fred's in Brighton, rubber soled canvas Comfort shoes, stolen Levi's, and a Mac Curtis T-shirt you had to send off for to somebody called Ronnie Weiser and that you wore under a check shirt. Steve Tardelli was wearing white T-shirts and low-hipped Levi's and reading poetry and talking about Tex Avery and Lester Young, but only Scott and Bombhead were skinheads. So when I saw Dawn with her white blonde feather cut, her tough boots and black Fred Perry, it was like she was somebody else. It was new to me and I started putting all kinds of crazy things together in my head. You know how it is when you're into someone. I never really have stopped thinking about her.

That summer there were so many skinheads they had their own beach, east of the Wish Tower and the Pier. If they hadn't slept there the night before, by the big beach fire they always made, the little skins like Gary Angelino and out of work skins like Eddie Beer would always meet there in the early morning to map out the day.

Gary Angelino rode a skateboard, and in the early mornings that summer you might have seen him skating to the beach from the two rooms he shared with his brother Tony in the run down Spartan Hotel out past the end of Seaside Road, way down east along the front towards Langney Point. Gary would pick up the little skinheads at the Regal Arcade and they would skate west along Seaside Road and turn south to the front. Their moon heads reflected like soap bubbles gliding past the windows of Italian ice-cream parlors, a walk-in bucket of blood tattoo place, a rock and rubber ring shop, fish and chip cafes. Smoking draw and skating past the washed down, still wet, shop doorways Gary Angelino and the little skinheads left tracks drying quickly on the warming pavements.

On the beach the skinheads would drink warm pop and Breaker and smoke Rocky and play football on the sand. They would run into the sea grinning like hot young dogs or just lie around listening to old school ska or rock steady or Sham 69 on Bombhead's beat box. Ten or twenty skins playing under the sun in fading cut-off Levi's and tanned to the max.

Sticky with coconut oil and sand, young local girls set up at the perimeter of the skinhead camp. The girls flat chested and smoking and giggling and mooning over the tough skinheads. You'd see Gary Angelino scouting them out in the mornings. Next thing he'd be over there squatting down on his bare heels in front of the girls because he was there to trade, and sometimes the local girls would rope in an out-of-towner and serve her up to

Gary in exchange for some Rocky. Monkey-faced Gary Angelino, blond and small and quick, a skater and boy thief and getaway driver at thirteen and dead now.

Monday to Friday Gary was Scott and Bombhead's eyes and ears. In the day Scott and Bombhead worked roofing together. They wore tough steel-capped day boots and tar stained cut-offs and they burned dark under the sun. Al Babe was apprenticed to a landscaping firm way out at Pevensey Bay. Tony Angelino was a panel beater up by Langney Point. The working skinheads came to the beach in the late afternoon to swim and catch up on the news and start in on the cold cans of Breaker they brought with them.

Sunday was the big day at the beach. The skinhead family met at Fusciardi's up by the seafront for frothy coffee and showing off, their boots shining like Fusciardi's chrome coffee machine and glass counters. The skinheads leaned on the big picture window so that old man Fusciardi shouted at them that they would break the glass if they weren't careful, which is what the skinheads wanted to hear. The game was to fall and lean against the window hard enough to get Mr Fusciardi out from behind his shining counter but not hard enough to break the window. The skinheads never went overboard at Fusciardi's because Mr Fusciardi let them sit for as long as they liked over a cup of coffee or a Fanta, and he packed out the jukebox with the Trojan and Blue Beat records they loved. Mr Fusciardi was a small, pressed old man scented with Bay Rum who dyed his hair a kind of yellow blond. He told me he used to get the Teds in there back in the fifties and maybe the skinheads reminded him of those days when he was young himself. When I did not live there anymore, and there were no more skinheads in the town, Taylor Beaumont told me that when he was tripping Gary Angelino had jumped through Fusciardi's big picture window shouting "Skinheads!"

Watched from a distance by out-of-towners the skinheads would fall in outside and parade in the sun

up to the seafront and down onto their beach. They
would shout and laugh and pick up beach stones and
throw them hard at each other. I would watch Scott and
Bombhead and the skinheads team-handed and
marching in the sun, and think nothing could touch
them.

I remember one afternoon Bombhead laughing and
saying look at little Gaz's harem, as Gary and three of
the little beach girls in flowered bikinis drifted in a giant
black inner tube towards the dark water under the Pier.
The watching skinheads arranged in ranks of rising
toughness up the beach, the smell of roof tar strong in
the air. I sat at the top between Scott and Bombhead
looking down at Al Babe, Tony Angelino, and Eddie
Beer. The heads of the skinheads looked hard like the
beach stones all around. All the tan baby skins played in
the surf like dark children of the king.

Most days I got there real early to swim, that was
always my thing and what I loved to do, but it was
never a surprise to find Dawn already on the beach. She
liked the early mornings before it got hot. Soon as the
sun was straight up and beating down she'd head for the
Wagon or inside somewhere else. I didn't always know
where she was. Sometimes she came back to my house.
Nights she'd want to party and that meant the Wagon
and then the beach.

Whenever I stayed overnight in the skinhead camp at
the beach she told me to always check my boots before
putting them on in the morning. She'd leave her tiny
half-sole monkey boots by the fire with a whole bunch of
others that might have looked like boots left outside a
sandy beachside temple except that these were all high
shined Air Wear, blood coloured or black and cherry
red, steel toe caps some of them, eight, ten, or twelve
eye. I wear flip-flops I said. Fucking check them anyway
Kim, she said, Tony brought a girl back here the other
night and Gaz pissed all over her stilettos. And the sea
air could leave salt lines and fuck your boots forever she
said. I thought then that she must have slept on the

beach most nights and it turned out I was right. Mostly
right, I should say.

I remember walking into the skinhead camp one
morning at low tide when she was standing on the
hump of a sandbank on the far away shoreline, bent over
and black as though sky-lined on a hill; from a distance
just a barefoot little kid in rolled up Levi's and training
bra. Under the early morning sun the starry rising sea
around the whale humped sandbank she stood on
glittered as though a lost city of gold might be found
below the surface. I watched her swimming back to the
beach when the water began to rise over her feet. She
swam all fierce and determined like a castaway trying to
reach dry land. On the beach she took off her Levi's and
let them dry in the sun. While they dried she scouted out
rock pools in her bra and black knickers. I watched a
couple of tan blond boys who looked like they might be
from Uptown giggling and tracking her across the sand
as she moved from little pool to little pool. The boys
began throwing handfuls of wet sand at her. She threw
rocks and stones at them. She hit one of the tan blond
boys in the face hard enough to draw blood. He ran
away holding his face and the other followed.

We were supposed to be careful about being seen
together. They only let me go home if I didn't see her. It
was something her Dad asked for. The social worker
they sent told my Mum she had no choice. That's what
they told me up at the school anyway. Back then I hadn't
learnt that what they told you was not always true.
What I thought had happened was that her Dad had
found out about us and made my mother send me away.
I guess he was good at playing the system which you
wouldn't have thought to look at him. He looked like a
dirty tattooed pirate. But then again I'm tattooed now,
like my friend Taylor Beaumont says, from arsehole to
breakfast time, and I've got daughters of my own so
who's to say? It was either the special school they were
going to send me to or somewhere worse. Dawn was
thirteen when we started which makes me fifteen, no,

sixteen, the summer I came back home. Scott's three years older than me. The next summer when I was seventeen Scott was still in prison and I did not live by the sea anymore, not then and not for years afterwards. She was thirteen so her Dad had the right but we were just kids.

Dawn was always a tough stray kid. She lived alone with her Dad above the repair garage he had off Seaside Road. He mended bikes and cars. He'd been in the Hells Angels but they'd booted him out for some reason. If Dawn knew why, she didn't say. It was after that they moved to our town. I saw her kicking around town on her own because that's what I was doing. If the sun was up I'd be at the beach but the rest of the time I wandered all over. I'd walk out as far as the Cuckmere Haven river valley and the Seven Sisters chalk cliffs in the west, or the wild Crumbles beachlands and Pevensey Bay in the east. The first time I met her was in the Regal Arcade on Seaside Road. The Regal was run by a dirty Ted called Mick Le Measurer. Mick sat in a wire cage teasing and stroking and greasing his red quiff that rose like a shelf. He made change and served up baby spliffs to the kids. I had Scott else I would have started off smoking with Mick probably, a lot of kids I knew did. Starting at the tip of the little finger on his right hand Mick had inch marks tattooed down the inside of his arm up to the elbow, and on his hands he had blue swallows that had faded and spread and looked like death watch beetles. Al Babe wouldn't go in the Regal because he said Mick was a poof and Al Babe was forever saying how much he hated poofs.

Dawn was playing pinball and bouncing smoke rings off the dirty glass. The table came up to just below her thin, pale shoulders. She had green eyes and a black Mohawk and red bitten fingers. She had half a dozen cheap nickel crosses and sleepers in her ears. I could hear gulls in the street outside. You could always hear them. She saw me looking at her and said, What are you fucking looking at? That kind of talk didn't surprise me.

If you didn't want to be taken for soft that was how you talked to people you didn't know.

That first afternoon in the Wagon Dawn said, "What happened to you up there?"

"Well, you know," I said, "Everything fucking happened to me up there."

I was carrying the weight a teacher called Anderson had put on me. He used to watch me swimming. He followed me all around and put his hands on me. I couldn't tell anybody about it then, not Dawn or Mum certainly, not Scott ever, and there's a good chance I won't tell you. Scott hadn't brought me up to be like that. I was supposed to be quiet and hard like him and not get used. Other things happened that summer that blasted Anderson out of my heart and mind, or so it seemed to me then. Now I see it's like the wolf who blows down the little pig's straw house. You have to make the connection.

THE PAINTED Wagon was a low, dark place kind of sunk down like a bunker on Seaside Road. It had blacked out windows. You had to step down when you came in to it from the street. A long room with a dirty lino floor and a narrow bar at one end was pretty much all it was. There were some chairs and a couple of tables, a Rock Ola jukebox, and a pool table with a torn blue cloth. A Maltese man called Gorgeous George owned it in name. During the day he stayed behind the bar drinking iced Remy, chain-smoking Dunhill's, and not saying much at all. George wore a crow black hair-piece and French cuffs on his shirts. Scott and Bombhead paid George off and did whatever they wanted. George didn't like it but there wasn't much he could do about it. George had some weight in the old days I guess, but Scott and Bombhead were the coming men. I heard that George left town after the summer.

At night a girl called Julie Spanish served up cans of Breaker and spirits in plastic cups. Scott wouldn't have glass in the bar after Al Babe glassed a Persian kid who'd come in by mistake. Julie Spanish had jet black hair kind of piled up and she wore lots of black eyeliner, short black plastic skirts, and torn stockings. I never heard her say much but I thought she was really pretty and Scott loved her more than anything. I know that because he wrote love notes about her and he never wrote anything down.

All the kids from our side of town used the Wagon and started off drinking in there but when I walked in Dawn was standing on her own by the ruined table playing a game of pool against herself. I didn't recognise her at first. She was still real small but her bleach blonde feather crop changed her. Her Pharoah eyes still shone brightly in a face that was splashed with freckles like my brother's, and she had red lips that looked painted but weren't and seemed so bright because she was always so

fair, even in the summer. She was never tan. I don't
know why but she didn't like it. Everybody else was
super tan. Dawn wore a black Fred Perry and skin-tight
Levi's that she had tie-dyed with bleach. Bombhead had
written Bombhead on them. Gary Angelino had his
name on there. Other boys had written other stuff on
her. She wore her tiny half-soled boots. I had a million
questions but I knew she wouldn't answer any of them. I
wanted to touch her all the time.

We sat down. To be saying something I said to her,
"How's it going with your Dad?" To tell you the truth I
didn't know where I stood with her. I say I knew where
she would be but I was hoping more than anything else.
I'd had no promise from her to meet up.

"Fuck off Kim, buy me another beer. Look," she said,
upending her empty can of Breaker on the table. She'd
found some money for tunes and *Train to Skaville* was
pumping out. She was bouncing up and down in her
seat to it.

There was rubbish on the tabletop. Empty Breaker
cans and silver paper. The ashtray was full. There were a
couple of burn marks on her hands. You never knew
how things were between Dawn and her Dad, she never
said. Dawn could keep secrets. I never could. I think the
Hells Angels pretty much told her Dad to get out of
wherever it was he was living then and from what you
hear about them he got away with it. The Angels are big
on the tattoo scene. The ones I've talked to are good
people but you wouldn't want to get on the wrong side
of them. Newhaven it might have been. People called
her Dad Dug and he was in his thirties. From what
Dawn told me I guess her Mum told him to clear out too
but Dawn was too little to really remember so you don't
know. What I haven't told you is that Dug was where
the drugs came from. It seems like I've always known
that but it's true that I can't remember when I first found
out. It explains a lot of things.

Dug sold Rocky hash by the nine-bar to Scott and he
sold to the Persians. The town was poor in the east and

33

rich in the west as the land rose to the South Downs. The territories of the skinheads, punks, Teds, and rebels then concentrated in little strongholds in the roads and small council houses east of the Pier and along Seaside Road all the way out past Langney Point to the wild beach lands of Pevensey Bay. Where the rich kids lived in the west was called Uptown.

The Persians controlled the centre. Kids from all over came into town to pick up at the weekend and now that Scott and Bombhead were trying to move in on the Persians that was where the action was. The Persians dressed in soft pastel Lacoste polo shirts and Benetton sweaters, pressed Fruit of the Loom jeans, and buff Italian slip-ons. The top Persian was a sleepy looking tough nut with a tall chocolate pompadour. His name was Hazim. There were two others who he took everywhere with him. One of them was called Ahmed but I don't know what the other one was called. They drove Hazim around town in a silver car. Gary Angelino told me that more than anything he wanted to steal the big silver car. Gary said thinking about ways to steal the car kept him awake at night. Tony Angelino said I can hear what keeps you awake at night you dirty bastard.

Al Babe said Gary had no chance. He said that the Persians wouldn't let anybody near the car. He said the Persians were set out in Uptown planning for the day when they would all drive big silver cars through our town. Scott said Al Babe was right. He said Hazim and the Persians wanted to keep the skinheads down in the east of town. He said they wanted to get our places raided and the skinheads busted one by one and locked up. They find you out there wandering around on your own at night like you do Kim, Scott said, the Persians will pick you up for sure because of who you are.

The skinheads hated the Persians and said it was because they kissed each other and held hands but I think they really hated them because they had money. I know that's why I did. I mean for us the fighting and hating was a way of saying you were in the world. I guess if you're a kid with money you get to do stuff that gives you a different kind of kick but I wouldn't know. Maybe your Dad's got a boat. With boys like us people just said no all the time.

I know a lot more about Dug now but I don't know how it got that he had Dawn and her Mum didn't. It made you wonder what her Mum was like. Dug's garage was on Seaside Road away from the beach in a part of town the tourists would never see or go to. The last time I'd seen him before I went away to the school on the downs he was standing in the yard of his garage with some kind of wrench in his hand. I don't know what kind. I was with my Mum and a social worker who was young like my Mum but not as tough. The social worker seemed scared of Dug. I don't know what her name was. I don't think she'd been in town long. She didn't seem to know about him. My Mum wasn't scared of Dug but she was scared of what the social worker could do. I always thought my Mum had no time for men but what it was I think now is that she was angry all the time. You wonder if the people who run off from things ever think about the people left behind. People tell you to not think about it and get on with your life but I can tell you it's not as easy as that. You get locked into being unhappy and when someone tells you that you can come out it's frightening. My friend Steve Tardelli says that when you put your feet on the floor in the morning you need to take the time to tell yourself that today you're going to be happy. What I can compare it to is when Steve is tattooing me and then stops. When he's tattooing me I have to find a way to live with it and when he stops it takes some getting used to how wonderful you feel.

There were two big chopped down bikes in Dug's yard and it was swept and clean except that there were oil spills on the ground. Dawn said you could see rainbows in them. Dug's forearms were black with dirt up to his elbows so that you couldn't see the winged Death's Head tattoos that Dawn had told me were there.

He wore dirty blue overalls and no shirt and steel capped boots. He had long black curly hair like it was still 1974 and a black beard and black dogs eyes that I couldn't see any light in when he spoke to my mother. His shoulders were humped with muscle. He wore gold sleepers in both ears. He had spider web tattoos, one on each elbow, and there was a Death's Head tattooed on the left side of his neck with AFFA written underneath it. Between the thumb and index finger of his left hand he had '13' tattooed, and in the same place on his right hand he had '1%'. Through the open door of the garage I could see a photograph of a black haired Dawn wearing just shorts next to a picture torn out from a magazine of a young looking girl with breasts that stuck out.

Dug moved slowly. He came across the yard and sparks came off his boot heels and he looked at us with his dead black eyes. He stood over my mother and when he spoke it was like a chopped bike starting up on a cold morning. Mum wearing the cut-offs and cheesecloth shirt she always wore in the spring and summer, her tawny hair long down her back, her brown arms folded across her chest.

"I can have the boy locked up," Dug was saying.

"No," my Mum said, "You can't. It's your word against the kids. Are you going to stand there and tell me that Kim's her first boyfriend?"

"My girl is wild it's true," Dug said, "but so are your boys. Kim's starting to act like his brother."

"Scott's got nothing to do with this," Mum said. She took a step forward. "Don't you talk about Scott."

"I'm just talking about what I know," Dug said. He stood with his hands folded inside the bib of his overalls. I could see the spider webs tattooed on his elbows. I felt like a little insect.

"Aren't you going to say anything?" My Mum said.

I didn't know if she was talking to the social worker or to me.

"Dawn's father is within his rights to ask you to make sure Kim stays away from her," the social worker said, "and what with everything else the school may be the best thing for Kim."

I remember standing in shade that raised goose bumps on my arms and looking up at the sky perfectly blue above his black roof as though the beauty of the day would be spoiled unless it was withheld from the place we stood in, and I remember Big Star's *Thirteen* coming from the tape deck of the dirty blue Ford he had up on bricks, but I don't remember hearing much more that was said. I was looking at the picture on the garage wall. I could always do that, just take myself away from everything. Now I think about my Mum. She was younger than I am now. She did everything on her own right from when she was twenty and my Dad left and then she had me.

Dug looked over his shoulder at the Ford. "I need to get back to work," he said. "I want the boy kept away from her."

"Don't you people know about him?" my Mum said to the social worker, as Dug walked back to the Ford swinging the wrench. The social worker started talking again and Mum took me away from there.

In the Painted Wagon I felt Dawn's head. It was soft and spiky and I left my hand there. She reached up and took my hand away.

"You don't seem that happy to see me," I said.

She shrugged and took one of my cigarettes from the packet on the table and lit it and inhaled.

"You are such a girl," she said. "Look at me. I'm a boot girl. I'm a skinhead." She kicked her feet.

"That hippy school they sent you too Kimmy," she said, "I don't know that it's done you any good you know, I mean, you need a hair cut." She looked at me with her head to one side and blew out smoke. "Definitely. And you're smoking too much."

She was right. I had let myself go. It was that kind of place. The school was on a hill and I could look out of my window there and see chalk downs, and if I stretched a little and if the day was clear I could see the

Long Man of Wilmington on his rise. I remember one
night a bunch of us going up there and painting a big
cock and balls on him. They must have known that it
was us but they never asked anybody. I think that
secretly they must have thought that it was funny.
Anderson told us that the Long Man was meant to be the
Anglo-Saxon god Balder, the second son of Odin and
god of the summer sun. When we were high in the
Wagon once I told Al Babe this and he wanted to know
where I'd heard it. Some people said that the long
straight staffs the Long Man held were for surveying ley
lines but Al Babe said he believed the story about Balder.
I just heard it, I said, what about you. Al Babe looked at
me funny. Back when I had long hair, he said, before I
was a skinhead. A long time ago. When I was still at
school.

On my first day Anderson had put his arm around
my shoulders and shown me the school. He made me
cold, as though he brought weather with him that was
always bad. I never got used to him and I think he knew.
He used to bring me things so I wouldn't notice. The
school was white and there was an orchard and there
were pear trees and some deer. To be honest, whenever
Al Babe went into one of his Keep Sussex White
speeches it was like this Anderson talking. I didn't think
it was unusual to tell you the truth. It would have been
surprising to hear anything different.

"Anything that you've done," he said, "anything that
you are ashamed of, I want you to forget about." He
looked at me then, still with his arm around me, and
then took me downstairs to where there was a
swimming pool. I'm not going to tell you what he
looked like.

Sometimes in the afternoons when I was high I
would walk through the gardens and the orchard and
out onto the downs. I would look for fossils in the chalk:
ammonites, sea urchins and sea lilies. I would read
sitting with my back against cool stone that somebody
told me was sarsen stone. I would watch the cloud

shadows moving quickly over the downs until it got dark.

Dawn always called it the hippy school. Even when she sent me letters she just addressed them to me, care of the hippy school. Some boys, I knew, had just been left at the gates of the school by their parents. These were boys who stayed the summer and for all I knew were there for years. I remember walking out through the sweet smelling orchard with my kitbag and looking back and seeing a face at a high window watching me leave. I could not be sure at that distance but I thought that it might be a boy called Buckingham. A small, pale boy who I had never heard say a single word. I heard him sing though. We had come into Assembly on a warm morning in late May and Buckingham was on the stage wearing sun faded Levi's and work boots and a white T-shirt. He had slicked his fair hair back. He had a story going on in his head for sure. Buckingham played a tan, shining acoustic guitar that looked too big for him and he sang this country song in a high voice. It was a song about love of course, about being so much in love it was like coming home, but it was a long time before I wondered who it was he had been singing about. We had all been taken away from people we loved.

A long gallery ran along and around the fourth storey of the schoolhouse. Our rooms were there and opened onto the gallery so that our rooms faced one another in the round. In the morning you would open your door and sometimes see the boy across the landing opening his door. The ceilings above us were painted with birds of paradise and monkeys hanging from vines. On the wall by my bed, next to the pictures of herself Dawn sent me, somebody, a teacher maybe, Anderson, had painted the words: burst joys grape on your palate fine. I didn't know what it meant then.

It got so I used the swimming pool in the basement only when I thought Anderson wouldn't track me down there. I love to swim and always have. The sea was not far away, out through the orchard and just beyond the downs, but I never saw it and I missed it. I wanted to swim deep and stay longer than my body allowed.

I discovered that I could not get down to the sea and back without being missed and somebody being sent after me. In my high room I listened to the waves breaking on the beach. The sound becoming louder and then diminishing like the unattended beating of my heart.

As Dawn and I sat and talked on that first afternoon, skinheads were coming into the Painted Wagon. Each boy was announced in the falling summer light as the door to the street opened. The boy standing in light so that for a moment the figure was blurred and gold edged and you could not tell who it was. When the door was closed the boys were pale in the restored gloom, and then, when you had become accustomed to the changed light, you could see that this was Al Babe, and this was Gary Angelino, and this was my brother Scott. They were tan not pale, and they were coming through the door that swung open and back and walking up to the bar cocky as teenage gunslingers of the long ago Wild West. Gunslingers with cropped hard heads and Foster Grant wraparounds, wearing Ben Shermans and Sta-Prest, Fred Perrys and Levi's, high shined boots and braces.

WHEN SCOTT saw me he smiled and when he smiled it was like the sun coming out. Yes it was. He was super tan from working up on the roofs of our town and from weekends at the beach. These big rock hard hands. His boyish freckles were almost lost to the darkness of his face. His penny red hair was sun lightened to a gold that matched the colour of his eyes. He wore shined up boots, tight sun faded Levi's, red braces, and a snowy white button down Ben Sherman with pressed sleeves folded to the elbow. He seemed about to burst out of these clothes that at the same time fitted him perfectly. On his right arm Scott had a new tattoo. A big Death's Head with jewels for eyes, *Straight to Hell* written underneath, and the cards of a Dead Man's Hand fanning out in back. When I looked at him I still saw a beach kid but he was getting harder to see. My brother flashed his sunshine smile. He saw everything in the pub without seeming to and shut the smile down to a cool hard look that was like the door to his heart closing.

I wonder now about the war Scott was fighting with himself and with the world because it was the same war we were all fighting. Boys like us I mean. Everybody was coming on all super-hard everywhere you went. It had come up on me slowly, this kind of life where you couldn't leave any soft part of yourself showing, but with Scott it came on him fast. I still believed that there were too many good things in Scott for them all to stay hidden the way he was trying to hide them. The sun showed in his face sometimes because Scott was nineteen and the boy was still in him. Scott hadn't closed him down all the way yet, but the first thing I remember about Scott from that summer is his smile. I guess because this was when it slowly began to disappear.

I watched the boys in the Wagon getting puffed up and showing off for him. It was just little things but if you knew what you were looking at you picked them up. The talk got tougher and louder for one thing and people were calling out to him. Skinheads started pushing and bumping off each other. Gary Angelino got into a smoke ring fight with his brother Tony. I knew all this was for Scott because it was how I was with him. You wanted him to notice you. It made you light up when he did. Only Dawn wasn't acting up any more than she always did. She had her own story going on and went her own way.

"You two really do look alike," she said as Scott came over, "I'd forgotten."

I stood up and he hugged me. I could feel my heart beating. Scott was filled out from roofing and his arms around me were enormous. I felt good when he hugged me, like I was really home. He whispered something to me. The sharp points of his crop rubbed against my face. I looked at Dawn's hair. I knew it would feel the same. Scott smelled clean as sunshine like he always did.

"Hello mate," he said to Dawn. His voice seems to have a lower register than mine and when I am with him, and afterwards, I hear myself trying to talk like him, my voice rumbling down to match his. My wife laughs at me about this and when I was younger other people who knew me, like Bombhead and Al Babe, did too.

"Horse," Scott said to me, "I didn't remember you were coming home today."

A long time ago Scott used to call me Little Red Horse because of my long red hair and because I used to fall over my feet when I ran.

"Yeah you did Scott," I said.

"How was it?"

"It was all right."

"I saw your stuff when I went home to get changed. You ran the place, right?"

I laughed.

"Seen Mum?"

"Not yet."

"Been swimming?"

"I meant to."

Scott looked at Dawn and laughed and put me in a headlock and rubbed his big knuckles over my head. He grabbed my hair and pulled it and wrapped it in his hand and made to scalp me. My red hair was down to my shoulders.

"Your fucking hair mate," he said, "It's got to go."

"Fuck off Scott."

I'd been reading a book called *The Outsiders*. All about this kid called Ponyboy. Ponyboy's got no Mum or Dad and he lives with his brothers Darry and Sodapop. Darry looks after them all. Ponyboy and his brothers are greasers with long hair. Ponyboy loves his greased up quiff. He says it's who he is. I felt the same way about my long red hair. Not even Scott could get me to cut it.

Scott let me up and threw himself into the seat beside us. We sat and for a little while we kept up the no talking talk that we did. We talked about boys we knew. Gary Ladd was inside again for fighting. Gary had been in half a dozen borstals and detention centres. This time he'd been sent to Lewes prison because he was over eighteen. Billy Downes was on the run somewhere in Hastings after knifing a Persian up by the Station Bar. The boy Billy knifed wasn't badly hurt, but of course he was rich, they all were, and his family had flown in from Persia-land and wanted to make sure Billy was caught and put away for ever. Billy wouldn't have a chance if they caught him Scott said. They'd bury him. The Persian had a knife too, Scott said, but nobody cares about that except us. Scott's golden eyes flashed. When Scott told me something I took it for the truth and did not question him.

I say they were boys we knew, Gary Ladd and Billy Downes, but really Scott knew them not me. I had heard of them the way I'd of heard of Scott if he hadn't been my brother. That was the way Scott was headed, becoming a boy other boys talked about in the town. Boys like Gary or Billy might nod at me if I was with Scott but otherwise they wouldn't see me. I told people at the special school that I knew them though. I told the robbing and fighting stories about Billy Downes or Gary Ladd or Scott like I had been right there with them. Like I was this hard kid you better leave alone. I lived off the glory of being Scott's little brother for a long time. It was better than being me. I loved Scott and I wanted to be like him. I was always scared somebody would find me out. Years later when it was too late I realised that nobody ever did think I was tough. It was all in my head. Scott would say that's where I lived, in my head, and he'd be right. That's what comes of being frightened all the time.

I asked Scott where all the skinheads had come from. I wanted to ask him about Dawn. I had not been able to stop looking at her. The way she looked, the skin-tight jeans and boots and cropped down hair, was driving me crazy.

He looked around the Wagon.

"Mate," he said, "they just started popping up all over."

"How come there are nothing but skinheads in here?"

"Well me and Bomb sort of decided."

I'd say that Scott knew but would never say that the boys became skinheads because of him and Bombhead cutting sharp through the town. They showed the way. Scott and Bombhead were boys who burned with fires inside that you believed could not be put out. If you were a skinhead that summer you were part of a family of boys that were looking to run the town. Scott had dreams of glory for sure. He wasn't just thinking to take out the Persians. He was looking to replace Dug. Mostly back then with me and Scott though, the things we didn't talk about could fill a book.

"Are you stopping?" he said.

I looked at Dawn. She shrugged and blew a smoke ring that drifted and kind of popped against Scott's shirt.

"Yeah," I said, "I think."

Scott looked funny at me and at Dawn smoking

down her John Player. Like Scott suddenly remembered
that Dawn was supposed to be my girlfriend and not
just some tough kid belonging to Dug who dressed like
she wanted to be Scott and who I was hanging out with.
She was still bouncing around. She never could sit still. I
should have asked her about the skinheads and what
was going on but I couldn't think straight. I just wanted
to pull those tight jeans off her.

"Maybe we'll go and come back," Dawn said.

"Yeah?" I said.

"Where's Bombhead?" she said.

"He'll be in later," Scott said, "You know how it is
with him. He goes where he wants to go. He'll be in
when it's time."

"Maybe we'll wait to see Bomb," Dawn said. "That all
right with you?"

"Sure," I said. I was surprised she asked me.

"I'll see you in a bit then Horse," Scott said. "All
right? I need to talk to you."

"Talk to me now if you want to talk to me," I said. I
was near drunk.

Scott half looked at Dawn. He looked at me and his
gold eyes flashed.

"Mate there's just stuff I need to take in hand," he
said. "You know how it is. I'll catch up with you later.
Look I'm really happy to see you Kimmy."

"I'm glad to see you too Scott," I said.

"Yes mate," he said.

Dawn had caught the look Scott had thrown out to
me.

"What was that about?" she said.

"Search me," I said.

Scott went over and put his arm around Al Babe who
was standing in front of the Rock Ola. He walked over
with his shined up boots pointed outwards and his
hands in his front pockets, his thumbs outside the
pockets of his jeans. Scott's Levi's had been hand washed
and sun-dried so often they were pale and soft. Together
Scott and Al Babe looked into the gold light of the Rock

Ola. Scott's soft pale jeans and plain white Ben Sherman became phosphorescent in the light of the jukebox. He was deeply tan from roofing, and standing in the light he was a form both dark and shining.

Al Babe started to put a coin in the jukebox and Scott quickly punched Al Babe on the side of the head and grabbed for the hand with the money in at the same time. The last time I'd seen Al Babe his hair had been halfway down his back. Al Babe laughed and got my brother in a headlock and got the coin in the slot. As Scott and Al Babe wrestled everybody was watching. All the boys and Dawn and Julie too. There was a pocket of quiet and then Derrick Morgan's *Tougher Than Tough* came chiming out. Al Babe let out a war whoop and shouted "Skinheads!" Scott put his head down and charged Al Babe so that his back smacked against the glass of the Rock Ola. *Tougher Than Tough* jumped and stopped and began again. Everybody in the Wagon sang the chorus when it came:

Rougher than rough, tougher than tough,
strong like lion, we are iron
Rudies don't fear, no boys, Rudies don't fear

Al Babe and Scott singing with their arms around each other and their eyes open, Al Babe fair and slender and sea-eyed, glowing with the beauty he was named for. You should have seen them. I could tell you that before he was twenty-five Al was sleeping on the beach and breaking into hotels for drug money and he was not beautiful anymore, but you might not believe me.

Bombhead showed. The door to the street opened and there was no light this time. Bombhead filled the doorway. He was dark and tough and wide. His black eyes were almond shaped and his black hair was cropped to a three and razor parted on the right side. His nose had been broken years back and not set properly and so he had the wide dog nose too like me and Scott. You could look at Bombhead and see somebody tough and for sure he put a wall up with the way he looked and moved. If you looked in his soft black eyes you saw something else. A sweet kid looking out from an opening in a fort he'd made to hide himself away in.

In the cold months of the year Bombhead's skin became yellow and dry like fallen leaves but in the summer he was a deep burned driftwood shining black. Years later I watch my wife's skin darken and lighten in just the same way as the seasons change, but she uses shea butter to keep her skin soft. Bombhead had nobody to show him how. He lived with his white Nan and in the winters, at least when I knew him, his skin was dry and grey yellow and sick looking. In the summers he used coconut sun oil so he didn't burn up on the roofs. The oil kept his skin shining but he never made the connection and why would he? It only comes to me now because of where my life has taken me. His Nan looked after him otherwise though. She fed his size. Bombhead talked the same as everybody else in our town.

When they were going at each other on the beach one Sunday I heard Al Babe say, Where *are* you fucking from Bombhead? Al Babe didn't believe you could have black skinheads. The two of them kept the peace pretty much, but when Scott was in a royal mood he would let Al Babe and Bombhead go at each other and even take sides against Bombhead, his best friend from always.

This is what Bombhead was like; he came straight through all the skinheads and made for me. He picked me up and hugged me.

"Hello Bombhead."

He gave me another hug and pulled me close so only I could hear. "Call me Neal," he said. "Only the tough nuts call me Bombhead. You're not a tough nut Kimmy."

"All these skinheads," I said.

"I know. It's bloody great. It's good to see you. Scott's been on about you coming home for ages."

That was news to me. I was still wondering what Scott wanted to talk to me about.

Bombhead and Donnie Orange were the only two black boys in the town. I say black but Bombhead was mixed race though everybody said half-caste back then. I never heard the words mixed-race until I met my wife and we had the girls. Bombhead always thought his Dad was black until one day his Nan told him his Dad had been an Indian. Years later Steve Tardelli tattooed the word ASIAN in three-inch high letters in a curving rocker across Bombhead's stomach. Donnie Orange was fostered and lived with a white family. That doesn't happen as much as it did, my wife tells me, but it still goes on. I was telling her some of what I'm telling you and she put down what happened to Donnie on his foster parents but I'm not so sure. You told me Donnie had a girlfriend called Pig, my wife said. That was true but Pig was her name before she started going with Donnie. They were Rockabillies. They used to drive around town in Donnie's pastel lemon Vauxhall Cresta with Confederate flags on the bumper and a sticker in the back window that said The South's Gonna Rise Again.

Scott and Neal were best friends for longer than I can remember. One summer when they were about twelve or thirteen we made bikes from parts we found or stole and when the bikes were finished we rode them west along the beaches and up past the Pier and the Wish Tower and as far as the beginnning of the South Downs Way. We left the bikes by a tea stand at the foot of the Way and walked towards Beachy Head up into the scrub that was spotted with raspberry and blackberry bushes. We climbed into a warm head wind and looked down on the town and the beaches and the lighted sea that had no end. Neal dared us to sit on the edge of Beachy Head. He sat on the edge and swung his legs backwards and forwards and called us chicken until we sat with him. I looked down at the boiling white sea and felt sick. Sitting there made me want to jump. Terns and wheatears glided below me on the up drafts the sea wind made against the chalk cliffs. After that I kept my eyes on the blue heavens above. I sat kind of leaning right back with just my feet over the side.

That must have been the summer Neal's Mum died and he went to live with his Nan. Neal was in our house all the time. Mum wouldn't have other people in the house so you know Neal was special. I don't know how you can say when something started but after he went to live with his Nan Neal was always out robbing and getting caught and going in and out of detention centres for it. He'd come out just the same as when he went in. Quiet, tough and smiling.

There was one place called Send he came out of when he was seventeen that changed him though. He was a skinhead by then. He'd got his long black hair cut off on the same day as Scott. I don't know what happened to him in there. I didn't know, I thought he'd just got into lifting weights. I didn't think how it would be for somebody like him, a black skinhead, in one of those places.

A year or so ago Taylor Beaumont told me that Donnie Orange had killed himself. I don't know, you can't help wondering. What did you know about black hair and black skin and how to look after it until you met me, my wife said. Neal and Donnie had nobody to tell them who they were or show them how to take care of themselves, she said. None of us did, I tell her.

When Neal came out this last time he'd got big and he stayed big and for a time he turned a crazy face to the world. Like a bomb or something had gone off in his head, somebody said, and it stuck. I was just keeping myself safe, he told me. People think you're mental in them places they leave you alone. He had a knife edge to his Sta-Prest and his boots were shined. He had built these walls around himself. He was a ranking skinhead and if you didn't know him you'd say that was all that mattered to him.

In the Wagon more skinheads were up from the beach or in from work and starting in on drinking and getting high. Everybody looked like they would burst if something didn't happen soon. I was looking around trying to make sense of this skinhead thing.

Boys I'd known forever were shouting at me and Dawn, saying hello, taking the piss, making to scalp me and buying me beers. The lighted air was thick with smoke and big talk. I knew every boy in the Painted Wagon by name. I knew them before they were skinheads. I knew their brothers and their sisters. I knew who was supposed to be hard and who wasn't.

We had all come up in the same places. Wild boys from the southern beach lands carrying names, many of us, of men we'd never seen and would never know. Where would we go when we were too old for the beach? If you wanted something more than a life spent beating panels or roofing you'd have to become an inlander and be lost to the golden light and the ever present far horizon out at sea. My wife says that because my ancestors were white and fought in the service of rulers I have no stories of rebellion, but she did not know me then, or how it was, and we were rebellious. We were poor and angry for sure but also it seemed to be part of living on the beach to question what people inland told you, and to look for a different way to live than the one they tried to force on us. The beach was where we grew up as boys and came into our wild selves. I didn't get it then. Now I think it was the never ending sea always there to show the way to true possibility if you would just look out.

The top boys like Scott and Bombhead, Al Babe and Tony Angelino, were cleaned up for the night and turned out to look good. Tony Angelino was kind of folded in his seat showing off the inside hem of his brand new white Levi's Sta-Prest. Al Babe was wearing a Ben Sherman the colour of a pale blue morning sky and he was over putting the word out about white power to Gary Angelino and the little skins. Everybody's boots flashed and shone.

The littler skins were straight off the beach. They didn't have new clothes unless they stole them. Gary Angelino and the little skinheads sat around sharing cans of Breaker and two-ing up cigarettes and watching

Scott and learning from him.

A tan, long-haired blond boy in Topsiders came in, slim and bare-chested and wearing a heavy silver watch and Fruit of the Loom jeans, and Bombhead went over to talk to him. Anyone who came in who wasn't known or who wasn't a skinhead Bombhead was straight over there. Scott stayed in his seat. He sent his black friend to give over the Rocky and take the money. Bombhead gave the boy what he had asked for and the boy tried a complicated handshake with Bombhead. Bombhead put his hands up gently as if to say forget about it and the boy left. The little skinheads smiled at the blond boy's curls and at the way he had tried to shake hands with Bombhead, but Scott's look was on them and they knew enough to leave the blond boy alone. The blond boy was a buyer and so the skinheads, who could not afford drugs unless they stole them or dealt in them, did not laugh about the rich blond kid until he was gone. Every few minutes the door to the street opened quickly to fading light and then closed again. Each time the door opened and a skinhead or a new buyer came in you remembered it was a summer afternoon.

LONG SHOT *Kick the Bucket* blasted out and skinheads in ones and twos broke out in fits of wild moonstomping, dancing on the spot with their knees and elbows pumping. The moonstomping turned into a free-for-all bundle until the floor of the Wagon was full of tan, moshing skinheads.

Gary Angelino was lobbing Breaker cans at his brother Tony. Tony was dancing and Gary was outside the mosh chucking cans. He'd throw a can and then bundle in with the rest of the skinheads. Cans were bouncing off Tony's head and he didn't know where they were coming from. Gary was always torturing his brother. When Gary was twelve he had gone with him when Tony left home and went to live in the Spartan Hotel. Tony was seventeen or so. His Mum couldn't hold Gary after his Dad left the scene. There was a straight ahead older brother living out of town somewhere, and a sister called Cairo. In their rooms at the Spartan the brothers built a metal frame to brace the door. Bombhead said mate you couldn't get in there unless they wanted you to, not the law or anybody. Tony makes out it's his place but it's purely Gary's world, everything he's got in there used to belong to somebody else but it's all Gary's now.

Dance Crasher kept the skinheads bopping and next thing I knew Dawn was over plotting with Gary. The two blonds looked right together. They looked like brothers. They were hunched down by the pool table tossing these beer cans and cigarettte ends at Tony Angelino and then leaping up and moonstomping away. Tony was big and sunburnt and slow looking. When Tony looked around Gary and Dawn were jigging up and down and grinning at each other. Tony was smiling too. I guess he knew where the missiles were coming from but he had Gary in view was the main thing. Gary might depth charge your beer with a wrap of speed when you weren't looking but if he was in the Wagon he

wasn't out stealing cars. That's how I reckon Tony
looked at it. Where Gary was wild Tony was just
regular. I mean he was as tough as anybody and a loyal
skinhead but mostly he worked eight hours every day
panel beating to pay the rent and give something to his
Mum. People said he was crazy letting Gary live with
him but where else was Gary going to go? This way
Tony could keep a look out for his little brother and take
the weight off his Mum. Tony would rather have the law
banging on his door than on his Mum's, and bringing
Gary into the skinhead family was smart too. Skinheads
like my brother and Bombhead could show Gary how to
behave. Tony knew that Gary was for a life outside the
law but there was no point being stupid about it. I
thought Tony was smarter than he looked. He looked
out for his brother and put him first was what it was.

Scott was right in the mix, stomping along and letting
little skinheads bounce off him. Gary and Dawn gave up
throwing empties at Tony Angelino and started in on
running full speed at Scott. They'd start by the door of
the Wagon and get a head of steam up and go charging
into Scott. Scott brick walled them and they went flying.

Just as soon as the stomping started it stopped. Scott
walked away to get more beer and that was the signal
for the dance to break up. There were beer stains all over
Tony Angelino's new white Sta-Prest. I watched him
shrug it off and start building a joint. He burned little
sweet smelling shreds off a small block of Rocky and
mixed it in the bowl of his hand with tobacco from a
stripped out John Player. Everybody was shouting. It
was about four in the afternoon.

Scott came back over and sat with me. He was
coming up all brick red and hot looking and I knew that
he was high. Scott had two sweating cans of Breaker in
each hand and he put them on the table and pushed two
to me. He ripped open a can and gulped it down. When
he was finished he threw the empty can at me and it hit
me in the chest. I threw it back harder. I hit Scott high on
the head and a spot of blood showed above his left eye.

Scott kind of glared and then he reached up to wipe away the blood.

"Shit Scott, I'm sorry. I didn't mean to."

Scott opened his other can and white froth spilled over the side. He blew it off and drank. I did the same. The lager was ice-cold and burned going down.

"Mate," he said, "for fuck's sake," and blew out a hard breath. He checked the cut again for blood and said, "Here, I've got something for you."

Scott dug out a big chunk of Rocky and some paper money from his jeans and gave me the hash and the money and said, "There you go Horse," he said, "Welcome home. Don't say I don't give you nothing."

We were drinking and so we talked. Scott asked me what it was like in the school and I said it was fine, really. He kept asking me and I said mate, you've asked me. He asked me what I was going to do now. I said that I hadn't thought about it. It's the summer now, I said, that's all I'm thinking about. We'll see after the summer, I said. He looked at me. I know it's the summer Horse but what are you going to *do*? I was still wearing the old cut-offs and flip-flops I had put on when I got home and the white T-shirt I had left the school in.

"Some beach action," he said, "right?" _

"That's right," I said, "I just want to sit in the sun, that's all."

"But it was all right up there?" he said.

"Yes mate, for sure."

Dawn came back all hot and took the last beer on the table and opened it and drank. Her tight jeans were sticking to her. I looked at the boys names written there.

"Where you been," I said, hearing the need in my voice too late to stop it.

"Talking to Gary."

"What about?"

"Fuck *off* Kim."

I was close to wrecked. I looked stupidly at Scott. Scott reached over and pulled my hair.

"What about this?"

"What about it?"

Scott looked at Dawn and said, "You'll have to cut it for him. I can't have him coming in here looking like that."

"He's not going to cut his hair Scott," Dawn said, "You know that."

Scott looked at me. My hair had grown so long I could nearly hide behind it. I couldn't tell if Scott was joking and that was new to me, that I couldn't tell. Was Scott tough for real now? Scott laughed and said, "You suck him off he'll do anything you tell him."

I remember one time Gary Ladd got out of the Detention Centre. Everybody looked up to him and thought he was tough because he'd been in there. We all went to meet him the night he came home. It was like he'd been away to a war or something. Gary Ladd said that Eddie Beer had put him in it so Eddie got a kicking and everybody had to join in. Gary Ladd watched to make sure we all kicked Eddie. This was on the front up by the Pier. We all stood under the lights of the Pier kicking Eddie Beer. I kicked Eddie in the head but I tried not to kick him too hard. He was clever, Gary Ladd, because not many people liked Eddie Beer deep down. Eddie gave people the creeps and Gary Ladd knew he could make us kick him. He made us scared not to.

Scott was like that, I mean from before he was a skinhead. He had that in him and he was never going to be on the ground getting a kicking, not like Eddie. Part of being tough like Scott or Gary Ladd is being able to say tough things with a clear face. Tony Angelino was a head taller than Scott and heavier too and once I saw Scott back him up just by talking to him. Tony couldn't man up to Scott and you could see it in his face. Scott just kept looking at him evenly, you know? He just talked to him and stared him down. Tony ended up not looking at Scott. He looked at the floor. Scott was so into being tough he was getting to be tough all the time. He'd changed in that way since I'd been away. It was like he couldn't help it now. He couldn't take off the hard mask.

Each boy in my town was connected with all the other boys in a secret constellation where the boys who shone brightest were the toughest ones. Maybe it isn't the same for boys with money but that's how it was with the boys I knew. If you weren't tough you were left in the dark or you ended up like Eddie Beer. Some boys like Steve Tardelli and Taylor Beaumont were brave enough to make their own worlds where there were different rules. It's funny, but it always seemed to me that the boys who wanted to be tough and shine bright had to turn out gentler and softer lights inside themselves; like Scott turning his smile off over time, or Tony Angelino not being able to come out and just say that he loved his little brother.

So the tough boys always seemed closed down to me in some ways but for a long time I wished I were like them, like Scott and Bombhead and even Gary Ladd. It was like they were more alive than anybody else, you know? And in my heart I was caught up in all that. What else was there to want to be? For boys like us the world outside our own seemed closed off but if you were tough, or if other boys thought you were tough, you could believe you moved freely in the world you found yourself in. You could make a name for yourself and I thought that must be better than always running scared.

I remember in the summer before I went away when Scott came home with his hair cropped down for the first time. It was a hot day and the windows and the kitchen door were open to our small back garden where Mum was reading on her old blue sun bed. The bed was stained dark in places with the Ambre Solaire sun oil she used. There were fat bees flying in the still air and I could hear grasshoppers. I had just come in from outside and I was drinking cold milk at the kitchen table and reading a Daredevil comic. Scott came through the open door changed and sat down at the kitchen table smiling. His skull was white against the rest of his face and his gold eyes shone. Scott had freckles on the bridge of his nose. I thought then that the new hardness of his head would take over the rest of him and I wondered, when that happened, if I would get too scared to look at him.

When we were boys in the summer Scott used to take me to the beach all the time. I mean he'd want to. Mum didn't have to ask him. The remembered feeling of being on the beach in summer is of being always in light. When I was starting out as a dive guide down near El Quosir, I was often sent down to tie our boat onto a wreck. In that part of the Red Sea the currents were strong and divers needed a rope to get them safely on and off the wreck. The newest guides were sent in to tie on because if you missed the wreck you would be bounce diving over a hundred feet two or three times and pretty likely to get bent. Once I was taken out from the dive boat in a little Zodiac and got in carrying the rope but as soon as I was in the water the current carried me away from where I knew the wreck to be. I went down a hundred feet but there was nothing there and so I let go of the rope and put up an SMB so the Zodiac could see me and I came up slowly in open water. All at once I was in the blue, with nothing but water above and below me and as far as I could see in any direction. Most often when you are diving you are oriented by the reef or the wreck you are diving on, by fish swimming past you or simply by the limits of your vision. Out in the blue you couldn't tell how far you could see because everything was blue. I only knew which way was up by watching the breath of my life rise in mercury bubbles to the surface. It was coming on for noon and when I was about twenty feet below the surface the sun met the water and the sudden light all around was like the light on the beach when Scott and I were boys. I almost thought I'd turn and see him there with me.

When we were kids we mostly stuck to the beaches east of town where we lived. They were shingle beaches but sandy when the tide was low. At low tide we would walk out for hundreds of yards with the sea no higher than our ankles, our feet sometimes sinking into soft muddy sand that you shouted to each other was

quicksand. No sound but the gulls and the water. The
sun hot on our backs.

Scott would sit on his sun-dried towel and look out
for me when I swam. He would hug his brown knees
and smoke, his eyes half closed against the sun and
tasting salt on his cigarette and on the tips of his fingers.
Sometimes in the late afternoon Scott would stand and
shaking off the sand and brushing his hair from his eyes
he would say he was going to dive. Scott would make
his way barefooted through the summer crowds to the
Pier. Among the people moving in the sunshine I would
lose sight of him. Then I would see him sky lined and
sitting on the blue pier railing above the sea. Slowly my
brother would stand and balance on the railing and then
he would dive, passing through the air more slowly than
I thought possible. As he stood on the railing I always
held my breath as though I were under water. It was just
a game I played. Sometimes I would have to let my
breath go before he dived, often when he was in the air.
Once I held my breath all through it, as he rose into the
sky and then fell straight and dark and disappeared into
the sea. His head when he surfaced was dark on the
water and the sun was in my eyes but I could see that he
was smiling, even so. The beach is where I live, the
water and the sky above and the light that's made, and
my brother's the same. Scott could try and bury that part
of himself deep down. He could chop his hair down and
put on a hard mask. He could write a new self on his
skin with his tattoo saying *Straight to Hell*, but I knew he
was turning himself into a tough legend so he didn't
have to show what he was feeling.

SO WHAT I mean is, I think Scott took the no father thing differently from the start. Than the way I took it I mean. First he was dreamy inside and then he was angry, but he had decided early on not to show if he was frightened about anything at all. I can tell you stories about things that happened then with me and Scott that seem to be about our Dad and maybe I will, but that's because I've thought about these stories for a long time and I've got to where I can tell them any way I want to. If I let it everything becomes about him after a time. For a long while that was what it was like. Starting around the time I was ten or so. I couldn't think about anything but my Dad, who and where he was and if he ran away because he didn't want me.

One night when I was a kid a man came to our back door. He had long fair hair damp with sweat. He lived in the house where the garden backed on to ours. I had sometimes seen him standing by his fence, looking at Mum as she lay in the sun. Standing at our back door his shirt was open at the chest and the skin there was red, as though he had fallen asleep in the sun. He had done some work in the garden for my mother. His own garden was overgrown and sometimes I could see beer bottles flashing in the grass.

Mum stood in his way wearing a T-shirt that showed her flat tan waist. She wore cut-offs and was barefoot. Her hair was wet and loose. The man stood with his shirt open, his eyes half closed. He stood putting his foot forward on the step and then moving it back again. He smoked a hand-rolled cigarette.

"I think I should be paid. I've come to get paid, that's all." The smoke from his cigarette was blue in the air.

"I've paid you," Mum said.

"You know," the man said.

We stood for a while, the three of us, my mother's hand winding my hair into curls.

It was still hot. I could smell roses, and the new cut grass. The man looked as though he would fall asleep where he stood.

"I've come to get paid," the man said again, trying to smile. Once more he said, "I've come to get paid." Mum just looked at him. I remember her face set in a brown mask so that you couldn't tell what she was thinking. The man looked at my mother again then walked across our garden and stepped over the fence into his own. Mum picked up his cigarette end from the back door step and put it in the rubbish.

In those days I didn't put these things together maybe like I should, although Scott would say I make too much of everything. One morning when I was really little I ran into my mother's room, and found a man asleep in her bed. His back was tanned and freckled and his hair, the colour of my toy bear, fell onto his shoulders as was the fashion then. His feet stuck out at the end of the bed. He turned, rubbing sleep from his eyes that were gold like my brother's, and said hello.

I have forgotten the man's name now but he wasn't my Dad. He drove us to the beach in a white sports car. I was sick. I don't remember if Scott was there but I guess he must have been. Mum rinsed my clothes in the sea while I sat wrapped in a red blanket. The man threw stones into the sea for a long time; the wind whipping his hair as his throwing arm went backwards and forwards. I didn't see him again or anybody like him.

These are the kind of stories that now seem to be about my Dad, but back when I was a really little kid I don't think I ever thought about him at all. That's maybe because I didn't know any better but mostly, I think now, because I had Scott. Scott took care of me from the start. He played football with me. He took me to the beach and taught me how to swim and how to snorkel. He taught me how to ride a bike. He tried to teach me what he'd found out about being a boy.

He told me that if you got into a fight you had to stand your ground no matter what. We stood under the burning hot sun in the small fenced-in garden and he tried to teach me how to fight. He said it didn't matter if the other boy was bigger than you or if you were scared or hurt or bleeding. He said it didn't matter if it wasn't fair or if there was more than one of them. He taught me how to make a fist so that you wouldn't break your thumb when you punched somebody. You know how to do that right? Everybody does. Your thumb has to be outside the index finger not tucked inside. He said hold a bag of pennies in there. That gives your punches more weight. Put something sharp between your fingers. He said that the only thing that mattered in a fight was to hit the other boy until they couldn't hit you back: nut him, kick him in the balls, stamp on his head, anything. He said that the fight wasn't over just because the other boy was bleeding or on the ground. You had to make certain they weren't going to get up.

He watched me try to throw a punch the way he had shown me. I'm left handed so I had to do the opposite of what Scott showed me. I sweated up and my wet hair swung into my eyes and stung me. My arms got tired from holding them up the way Scott showed me. I threw a punch and tripped over my feet and fell over and Scott looked down at me and waited for me to get up. His face was dark with the sun behind him. I wanted to stop and go inside and read but Scott said it was more important that I learnt to fight. Mum watched us through the kitchen window. I couldn't tell what she was thinking. I understood everything Scott told me on one level but when it came to it, as it did sometimes, I kind of froze up. I say sometimes but really it was only the once.

We were at a beach party at the foot of some chalk cliffs one summer night. I was there with my friends Taylor Beaumont and Steve Tardelli. I'll tell you more about Taylor and Steve later because they are a big part of this whole thing but this story is really not about them, not yet. They were just who I went to the party with. I went everywhere with them before I was sent away. Everybody was really drunk and off it with Rocky

and downers so I can't remember much about what
happened or even where the party was really. I just
remember these chalk cliffs flashing with seams of flint,
but then there's miles of coastline like that where I come
from so you don't know. I remember these great pieces
of chalk that had fallen from the cliff and were lying on
the beach and along the changing shoreline and in the
slowly falling tide. Where the chalk fell you could find
the fossils of animals that lived millions of years ago.
Was the place called Sugar Mountain? Something like
that.

I remember the sunset came late in the evening so it
must have been in the high summer, mid-August, and I
remember the chalk becoming pale pink and peachy and
then blood orange before becoming violet and then
almost invisible and looming in the dark. And all those
colours were in the cliffs above and behind us and went
into the sea going away to the far horizon as well.
Seagulls and jackdaws and skylarks flew high above us.
Taylor said you could hear skylarks singing above the
sound of the waves and Steve and I listened. When you
really listened you heard so much you couldn't be sure
what you heard. The moon rose above the sea. The
moon was super fat and we all saw what we wanted to
see in it. That's the whole point of beach parties though,
right? Everybody gets fucked and goes, wow, look at
that.

Scott and Neal were there, before Neal was
Bombhead. This was when everybody was a punk pretty
much except me and Taylor and Steve. Because of his
brother Ted, Taylor was into his Rockabilly since he was
ten or eleven. Steve always went his own way when it
came to clothes and music. I remember Scott was
wearing some kind of combat jumpsuit and his hair was
spiked and he had steely boots on. There were people in
studded leather jackets and ripped up shirts and combat
bondage trousers dancing on these peachy pink and
orange giant pieces of chalk. Everybody was there really,
it was a big party. I didn't know half the people. I

remember everybody knew about it and was talking
about it weeks before. Dug was there of course, like
always. He'd turn up at every beach party with a beat
box and some acid. When Dug was around you'd hear
the Beach Boys or Hawkwind drifting across the beach,
and if you wanted the drugs he had you'd make for
those sounds, sometimes losing your way as the music
vibrated against the cliffs, the sounds going in and out
like the changing tide.

Dawn must have been there too but I can't say I
remember. She'd have been eleven so I maybe wouldn't
have noticed her. I say that, but she was never big on
sitting on the beach and staring at the moon and the sea
for hours. Dawn hated the Beach Boys. She was in my
room once when I put on my Mum's copy of *Twenty
Golden Greats* and Dawn took it off the player and threw
it against the wall and broke it. I didn't connect it to
anything important. Busting my stuff was just the kind
of thing she'd do. I thought it was because she was a
punk. When she got to be a skinhead I knew better than
to put anything like that on when she was around. All
she listened to was ska and rock steady, and Prince Far I
and Scientist when she was high. She'd do anything for
Scott and Bombhead but Dawn was so pure about her
music she didn't even listen to Sham 69 and Scott and
Bombhead loved Sham. I mean they could see through
the music but they loved the way Jimmy Pursey seemed
to be talking about their lives. She was a proper
skinhead Dawn. Of course I can't listen to the Beach
Boys anymore. I'll still sometimes dream of Brian Wilson
singing *Caroline No* and I'll wake up shouting and my
wife will have to hold me until I can speak.

In the gathering rosy dusk people collected
driftwood and beach rubbish and made big bonfires.
And there were girls there too. I had to find out about
girls for myself. Scott hadn't taught me about girls, he
never talked about girls the way other boys did. It was
always Julie with him. He cut his wrists deep enough to
bleed badly once, when he thought she'd been with

somebody else, but I can't tell you about that because Scott wouldn't want me to. This was when they first got together. When they were punk rockers.

I was really pretty then. I was. I was thirteen. I had long red hair, not as long as Al Babe's but long, and I used to wear Falmer jeans and a white T-shirt and basketball shoes. I've got really dark eyes and I was always really tan in the summer and my red hair showed the sun in it. Mum was pretty too, that's where me and Scott got our looks from. Long dark red hair and brown eyes with gold flashes in, cut-offs, a nice smile and a turned up nose. And she was young too when we were little. She was seventeen when she had Scott so that makes her twenty when she had me. I guess we kept the men away after that. She was a super tan beach girl in the summer. She'd spend all her time off there as soon as the days started getting warm. That's where I get the love of it from of course, Scott too. I think we forget that sometimes.

At the beach party there was this little blonde girl with big green eyes and wearing cut-offs. In the moonlight her long blonde hair was sea green. She was about my age and pretty too, and we were looking at each other all night until in the end she came and sat with me and we watched the fiery sunset together and shared a joint. We were holding hands and then we started kissing and getting hot and then this boy she had come with, this big seventeen year old from Uptown in a soft and pale blue Benetton v-neck and Fruit of the Loom jeans and Topsiders, came out of the dark breathing sweet hot Southern Comfort all over us and pulled me off her. I tried to remember the stuff Scott had told me but like I say I froze up. I couldn't make a fist or throw a punch. I was holding my thumbs inside my hands. I could have picked up beach stones and thrown them at him, but while I was thinking what to do he was beating me up, punching me in the head until I was down on the hard stones and bleeding and then he was kicking me when I was down.

Scott came for me of course. From somewhere beyond the big dark beach boulders. He must have heard me crying out. Scott was just sixteen then and not as big as the boy who was beating on me but he was all over him straight away, stamping on him until I thought the boy's head was going to disappear under the beach stones. Scott punched the boy with his hard hands. In the dark the boy's blood was black and thick running into the stones and he puked up the sticky sweet Southern Comfort onto a clump of purple green sea kale. A black headed tern coasted in and began to eat the puke. The boy turned to lay on his back on the beach and he made no sound. There was blood on his blue sweater. Two of his friends took him away. The big eyed blonde girl went with them, biting her fingers. Scott disappeared. I got drunk and burned my hand in the fire and woke up alone on the beach.

SCOTT KNEW so much about this stuff. And it wasn't until years later that I wondered where he'd learnt it all. I had Scott, but who did Scott have? Now I think violence may have come to him easily because he was so angry. I mean Dad left before I was born but Scott was three. I think he remembers. Of course he says he doesn't. When he was high once and we were talking I pushed him on it until he moved his drink away and folded his arms across his chest and said, look, I've tried but there's nothing there so whatever you think you know you need to think again. I would have told you, he said. Still it's hard to give up the stuff you hold onto that helps you make sense of things.

When Scott was a little kid he was really sweet looking and because for a long time he was sweet at home, when I started hearing stories about him from other boys I knew in town, like Tony Angelino, I didn't believe that they could mean my Scott. That he was getting into all these fights, starting them too, and robbing shops and houses. I know he never went to school. Scott had this surf splash of freckles across his face. He had hair that was bright and red and clean looking. He made people smile to see him. We both did. It's funny, I talk about his smile but I always thought he had a girl's smile, a smile you had to read and wonder about. He seemed to think about smiling like he was worried whatever it was that had made him smile was going to be taken away. With me I'd smile if I was happy and I'd be smiling before I knew it, it wasn't something to think about even if I could. I'm like a dog that way. Like I say Scott smiled a lot then, don't think he didn't, and his gold eyes shone when he smiled, but when I think about it now I don't know if he ever let happiness in him all the way. He never put a name to it and said it was his because he didn't want to have to give it back. He kept his guard up in a way I never could.

That's why I said I think he remembers. If he does though you'll never get it out of him. Whatever it is Scott sees when he thinks of Dad it's buried deep at the bottom of him. So don't ask him, that's what I've learned, because you'll just fuck him off if you do, and more than likely the next time you hear from him it'll be from a different country far away. You don't think about these things when you're a little kid though. I just thought he smiled like a girl. All nice and mysterious.

I didn't know how angry he was until he started showing it at home in little starbursts far apart at first, and then all the time as he got older, until he couldn't be at home. It was like he was blaming Mum for something, and because I didn't think about Dad at all then, except in this sense of a heavy absence, something that wasn't there but wasn't there all the time like money, I didn't get what he was blaming her for. He didn't come out and say it. I just saw this angry boy, the hero brother I loved, shouting at my Mum until she cried. And then he would go out and not care that he got into trouble because nothing that happened to him out there could make him feel worse. And sometimes because I loved him and wanted more than anything to be like him and to be brave like him I joined in. Mum didn't cry often, not in front of us anyway, because she was tough. She'd be more likely to tell us to get out and leave her alone for a bit. So when she did show it all, when she cried and let you see it, you knew there was nothing good about it at all. She'd put on her Carpenters records and smoke cigarettes and she wouldn't talk or even look at us. It used to kill me and if I had to bet I'd say it killed Scott too but he was already teaching himself not to show anything. Scott learned to hide his heart early is what I'd say.

I'm putting everything on Scott but I'll say one thing about back then. Scott never said to me this is the way to be Kim. I mean I learnt from him because he was my brother and there was nobody else around but Scott didn't talk tough. I never heard him talk about fights he had and the things he'd done and how hard he was. He never talked like that. That was all me. Everything he taught me was to help me. Scott had discovered that the world was tough and the thing to do was to be tough right back.

Another thing I can't put on Scott is that I never needed any reason to steal, especially after I started school. Scott sort of went to a rough, wild school near where we lived where the boys were fighting all day but nobody had money. I went to a different school to Scott because I was supposed to be clever. At the school I went to, in Uptown, and then at the school on the downs, I met boys with money and so for the first time I realised we were poor. I say that but when I was little I stole fountain pens, watches, knives, all these shiny birthday boy things I always wanted but never got and didn't know I didn't need.

At school I stole things because I wanted what the other boys had until I found that I couldn't steal their big houses, the big cars they were driven to school in, their holidays, their racing bikes, the way they looked at me when they spoke to me, the way they spoke. I couldn't steal their Dads so I started stealing their money and then I started stealing everything they turned their backs on. Half the time the rich boys didn't seem to notice the things I stole. They had so much. What I wanted was to be able to take the things to school and say that my Mum had bought them for me but I couldn't do that. Sometimes at night I got a knife or a watch out to look at but mostly I had to keep everything hidden out of sight. In the end I threw everything away and soon after I started being friends with Steve I stopped stealing. I still have to keep myself from taking things though. When I was about fourteen or so I went to a lot of parties in big houses in Uptown and I used to piss on the clean floors or puke up on the thick carpets on purpose. Crazy really, my Mum cleaned those houses.

Thinking about it now I wonder if maybe I was sent away because I was stealing. I didn't think anybody knew. I tell you what's strange. The way you know something's wrong when you're a kid but you don't have the words for it. To say what it is. In that house you had Scott with his hurt girl's smile building up to explode inside and me stealing knives and everything. What did I want with knives?

No wonder when somebody told her about the school on the downs Mum wanted me to go there. It might be that I've mixed up going to see Dug and going to the special school in my mind. That's maybe how it was, or it could have been everything all together, Dug and Dawn, the stealing, Scott getting wilder and wilder, and getting tattooed with skulls and death wishes written on banners.

It was Mum's life that was going out of control in all that. Me and Scott still had time to turn things round but even if we did it might just be too late for her. She needed things to start going right somewhere soon. With Scott I think she believed that he was gone away and that there was nothing left to do but wait and see if he ever came back, even if it took years. Plus I know she thought he was braver and tougher than me and that whatever happened to Scott he would be able to stay pretty much the same. With me I think she thought she could stop me before I went all the way out there and got too badly hurt. She needed me to come back from that school changed into her idea of me. I didn't think I was man enough to carry that weight, and sure enough there I was on my first day home drinking Breaker and getting high with Dawn in the late summer afternoon, and watching Scott getting some of his own back by serving up drugs in a skinhead bar.

I SAT on my small hard bed with Dawn. It was later. She had said to Scott that we might leave the Wagon and come back. I had kept close to her after that. I wanted to hold her to the promise I believed I had heard her make. Dawn did look just messed up enough to come back with me. Her shirt was wet with sweat from where she had been dancing. Her feather cut was wet and the smell of ice cream was strong in her hair. Dawn was setting fire to bits of silver paper. Then she started holding the lighter under her hand for as long as she could stand it. When she got like that she'd do anything pretty much.

After we had finished the Breakers Scott had bought for us I came on to Dawn strong and pestered her until she said all right she'd come with me. At my house the sun had begun to fall in the late afternoon and my bedroom was blooded with red light from the west. Mum was not home from work. I was in a big hurry and made Dawn keep on her little six-hole black half-sole monkey boots with white laces. Her black knickers came down with her jeans. Her jeans were so tight, I had to pull hard to get them down. Her black Fred Perry was on the floor.

Dawn lay back with her milk white legs open and her boots black on the bed, her feet held together by the boots and jeans round her ankles so that she was diamond shaped on the bed. The veins showed in her skin like blue rivers in the snow. The hair on her head was the only hair on her anywhere. She lay with her hands behind her head and looked at me with her green Pharaoh eyes. All the time I was in that place up on the downs I hadn't thought about much else but this. That is, after Anderson and going home, Dawn was what I thought about hardest. At night, with the painted paradise birds flying high in the shadows above me, I had held tight to myself and watched through the pictures in my head of the few times we had fucked. That was the strange thing, we'd hardly done it at all

70

before I got sent away. We were about more than that when we started out but it seemed to be everything to me now.

She was on the bed putting a finger inside herself. Come on then, she said. I couldn't get started and she reached for me, laughing, and began to jack me off like it was nothing to her, and then she moved onto her hands and knees and took my hand to touch her and as soon as I felt her it was fine. When she went on her hands and knees I got excited and she held me and helped me put it in. I held her thin ribs, her soft cropped head. I was sweating in the red light. The heels of her black boots were cold and hard against my thighs.

Afterwards she told me that she'd been at the party on the beach the night before and fucked three boys. She fucked them, she said, they didn't fuck her. There was a difference. In the heat of the red room I could smell us.

"Bombhead gave me some speed," she said.

"What else," I said.

"Breakers," she said, "I was drinking Breakers."

"Did you fuck Gary?"

"Who?"

"Gary Angelino. Did you fuck him?"

"I don't think so, I don't remember."

"Fuck off."

She was laughing at me from behind her hand. Her red mouth was open.

"Who did you fuck?"

"I'm not telling you," she said, "It's none of your business. You were gone. Besides, what do you care as long as you get a ride now?"

I got off the bed and picked up my cut-offs from the floor and got the chunk of Rocky that Scott had given me and a cigarette and dug around in the kit bag I'd carried my books and clothes home from the school in and found some rolling papers. I burned off the hash and built sitting on the edge of the bed and looking at her. She was so small she looked far away. I was trying to figure her. We hadn't done it a lot and we'd never done it that way before. I was tired. Everything that I had felt inside of me, all of the built up energy I had carried home to her from the school on the downs, was suddenly blazing back at me from her jewel green eyes and I could hardly stand up.

The room Scott and I shared became blood red on summer nights. The room looked out to rough land behind the single row of small houses that backed onto ours. The land went away to train tracks and at night I would listen for the sound of the last train going away up to London. There was a fireplace and sometimes in the night a lost and frightened tern would fall down the chimney and fly into the room. The bird covered in coal dust and beating its wings against the window. My bed was under the window and Scott's bed was against the far wall but there was only one night that summer that we both slept there. I had no pictures above my bed but Scott had put up a poster from *Enter the Dragon*. Redness came down the walls and soaked into Bruce Lee watching over us as the sun fell. I smoked and after a bit I said to Dawn, "Scott knows I won't cut my hair. Why does he say stuff like that in front of everybody?"

She pushed me down onto the bed and sat across me, holding me down on the bed like Scott used to when we were little, her arse and everything cold against my stomach.

"You have got to stop being such a girl, you know?"

"Don't call me that."

"Why, what are you going to do? What if my Dad comes in the Wagon and finds us?"

"I don't know," I said, "what if he does?"

"You don't want to know Kim," she said. "I don't even know what you're doing with me. How long do you think it'll be before he finds out you're back in town and that I've been seen with you? Do you ever think what will happen to me? Why don't you get yourself a girl from the beach and leave me fucking alone?"

I tried to sit up and she pushed me down again. She must really like me, I thought, and then I wondered if maybe she was only seeing me because her Dad didn't want her to. Her breath was sweet and hot on my face.

"What is it, am I the only girl who'll give you a ride?"

"It's not like that," I said. When I was around thirteen I started going with beach girls. I liked dark girls with long hair. There is something pure about a pretty tan girl in a bikini on the beach. I loved to sit close by them and just talk about nothing. All that hot brown skin close enough to touch, sticky with sand and broken shells, made me come near to popping. Proper beach girls always have a faraway look in their eyes, just like the boys. We spend half our lives looking out to that far horizon. There was one girl called Kelly with straight black hair that she wore free falling down her back. Kelly was brown already and in the summer she went South Seas dark. I remember the deep sun blush in her face and her swollen lips after we kissed. I remember the sweat and salt in her hair and her sun and salt faded black bikini damp under my hand. The hottest parts of her skin were the parts she hid from the sun. I remember the red marks the beach stones made on our bodies.

After I started going with Dawn, girls like Kelly wouldn't come near me. Kelly said, "She's a freak." Kelly said she went with me because I was sweet looking but if she'd known how boring I was and what a freak I was she wouldn't have. "All you want to do is kiss me and look at me and read books. All the girls think you're cute but I've told them what a freak you are."

After Anderson I didn't think I'd be able to talk to the girls on the beach even if they would talk to me. I was scared of new girls now. I thought they'd find me out and I didn't think I'd be able to do it with them. I had come close to panicking and not making it with Dawn. If you want to know the truth, not been able to make it with her was all I'd been thinking about since I'd left the school in the morning. So you're right, I was using her, but like I say how much time do you spend thinking about other people when you're sixteen? I needed to know that I was normal, so Dawn was right. She was the

73

only girl I knew who would give me a ride.

When we'd started going together there was a strong connection between me and Dawn. I don't know why. She was a tough punk girl and I was me. We both liked to roam around and Dawn didn't mind it when I told her stories from books I'd read. She liked it even. I don't think many people understood it when they saw us together. Like Donnie Orange and Pig. Two outsiders maybe or just lonely. She might have been the first punk girl I knew. I was looking for someone strong and I thought she was strong because she didn't measure herself against beach girls like Kelly. If she did she kept all that inside. Like I say she kept away from the beach when it got hot and maybe that was why. I always thought Dawn belonged in a city.

I looked at Dawn's pale, thin arms. She had some marks on her where I had cut her and where she had cut herself. I had them too. That was something we were into before, something we shared. I didn't tell you that. We had cut each other on the arms. It was after the first time we'd fucked, down on the beach on another red afternoon. Dawn had a short diver's knife she stole from her Dad. I had some bits of candle. We lit the bits of candle and smoked a joint. She'd cut herself before. I hadn't. She put a cross on me first and then I cut these three marks on her that looked like a K. The knife burned going in. We kissed for a long time afterwards and let the cuts bleed. We mixed our blood together with candle wax.

I think that before I went away she believed in me and that was a way to show trust, you know? It was how I felt about it when she did it to me. Things seem strange when you write them down but it didn't seem that way at the time. It was just what we did to show each other we meant what we said. I didn't think she'd let me cut her again. Not after I'd let them send me away. She knew for sure that she was stronger than me and she needed somebody strong. Plus she had the skinheads to believe in now. I wouldn't have minded if she wanted to cut me again though. I smoked the thick rough hashish and tried to put things together but the ideas floated past one another and I couldn't always see the connections. The scars were still there though and I remembered the blood. I still had my piece of bloodstained candle wax somewhere.

I didn't want to think about what Dug would do if he caught me with Dawn. When we started I didn't think about him because I didn't know anything about him. Up in the school he had been a monster in my head and I thought that I would try and stay away from Dawn. Now that I had been tight inside her again I knew that I'd come back every time she let me. Still he floated in behind my eyes with his dirty Rocker's face and halo of black curls. The gold flashing in his ears and his voice when he spoke to my mother kind of all wrong and disconnected somehow. I remembered the way he flipped the wrench he carried like he wanted to throw it at me as he walked back across his yard that was full of shadows.

Scott was buying from him. Dug had the edge because nobody knew who his suppliers were. So Scott and the Persians had to go through Dug or find another source. Dug would let the skinheads and the Persians fight it out and put the price up for whoever was left standing. Now Dawn was a skinhead and close to Scott Dug must have wondered what that meant. And if I was back in the picture it would be easy for him to see a plot building.

"Are you going to stand up to my Dad?"

"Scott won't let anything happen."

"That's what I mean Kim," she said, "You can't hide behind Scott. Don't you get it?"

I didn't say anything. I thought about what she said and didn't get any answers. Maybe she was giving me another chance. I couldn't believe she got anything special out of me that she didn't get from the other boys she said she slept with. Still she let me come inside her so what did that mean?

She pulled her jeans back up and buttoned them. I looked at her jeans. Were the names written there the names of the boys she slept with? Was that what the names meant? I flashed on her with Gary and maybe even Bombhead. That was crazy but it didn't matter. I knew she was one of those girls who would say things to get me started and see what I would do, but after the pictures were in my head it didn't matter if she was telling the truth.

"Hey," she said, and reached for the burning joint, "Give me some of that."

Like I say I read a lot. I've always loved to. Buckingham was the one who gave me the book *The Outsiders*, up at the school. He came up to me in the orchard and handed the book to me without saying anything. I sat up all night to read it the first time and when I finished it I started to read it over again. I thought that this boy Ponyboy who told the story was just like me. Maybe that's because Ponyboy seemed to be telling the story of my life. The way Ponyboy talked became mixed in with the voice in my head. Ponyboy's life was how I wanted mine to be, and that might sound strange when you hear about it.

Ponyboy is a greaser who lives with his older brothers Sodapop and Darry. They have no parents and Darry looks after his two younger brothers. Darry was a roofer like Scott. Ponyboy says that Darry is always rough with him. The greasers are poor kids who wear white T-shirts, jeans, and boots or basketball shoes and leather jackets and have long greased up hair that they love. They are always fighting with the Socs. The Socs are the Socials, the rich kids from the West side of town who drive Mustangs and wear Madras shirts. Ponyboy hates fighting but he can be tough when he has to be. He's smart too. He's a dreamer who likes books and movies and sunsets.

Ponyboy's best friend is called Johnny Cade. Johnny is always getting beaten up at home and running away. What Johnny and Ponyboy are really mad at is being poor and seeing no way out. One night Johnny stabs and kills a Soc who's drowning Ponyboy in a fountain and Johnny and Ponyboy run away and hide out in an old Church. They cut their hair and Ponyboy dyes his blond. You'll have to read it if you want to know everything that happens but later there's a fire in the church and Ponyboy and Johnny save some kids from burning but Johnny is burnt up and dies. So they're heroes and nobody has to go to prison. Ponyboy writes a story for school about it that becomes *The Outsiders*.

You know how when you look at someone when the sun is in your eyes on the beach or somewhere and their face is dark and gold lighted at the edges? That's how Ponyboy makes the story. It's a dark story but there's all this light in it at the edges. Ponyboy wants the golden light but there's all this darkness. His parents were killed in a car wreck and later on in the book you see how scared Darry was that Ponyboy and Soda would get taken into care. There are other bad things that happen too. Dallas Winston, he's the toughest kid in the book and he's the one who helps Johnny and Ponyboy get away, Dallas gets shot and killed by the cops. I loved that book and carried it all around. I guess because it had a happy ending. For Ponyboy anyhow.

On the beach the golden light was there for you all the time. The dark places were inside or at least they were for me. And that's what I was trying to tell Scott. I just wanted to sit on the beach and get that sunlight inside me until I was full. I knew that when I lay on the beach the sun would first be on me and then inside me, shining on all the dark places and breaking up the darkness until I was light inside again. I wanted to come away from the beach in the late afternoon and feel clean and new like when I was a little kid and had moved with the sun in me always, or so it seems to me now.

I knew it wouldn't last but like I told Scott, I wanted the summer. I thought it would help me sort everything out. You can call that running away or not facing up to things if you like but I knew that if I had the summer then whatever happened to me afterwards I'd carry some of the light it gave with me forever.

Now things were pushing in on me. She was telling me how I had to be and how I'd messed up in ways that seemed important to her. She had the skinheads now, not just me, and there was all this with Scott and Dug and whatever my brother wanted to talk to me about. I wanted to push all that to the back of my mind. I just wanted to wait and see whatever was going to happen next.

"Hey," she said, "don't fall asleep. Let's go out."

"All right," I said. I wanted to get out before Mum came home from work and found us.

"One day you'll tell me what you're thinking about all the time," Dawn said.

"Are you still my girlfriend," I said, "or do you belong to the skinheads now?"

She cuffed me fast and hard around the head. She was always hitting me.

"I'm a skinhead," she said. She stuck her hand down her jeans. "I'm still wet." She stuck her fingers under my nose. That was the only answer I was going to get.

"Can I write my name on your jeans then?"

"Only skinheads can write on my jeans," she said, "and whatever you are," she pulled my long hair, "you're not a skinhead."

She did a little war dance in front of me and laughed. She let me pull her close and kiss her. She had these tiny islands of brown skin on her shoulders where her freckles were joined together, these sweet inlets and harbours. I kissed her there and kissed the raised scars I had made on her skin that were like tiny sandbars. After a bit she pushed me away.

"Oh Kim," she said, all soft for once, "it's just fucking."

I pretended I didn't hear her. I should have asked her questions. What had happened. Why she was a tough skinhead. Why she wanted to be in a gang. What was she trying to hide. My way was to not think about things. It made it easy to believe that nothing bad was going to happen. The voice in my head though, I couldn't turn it all the way down. Dawn had waited to see how I would be when I came back. She thought I'd come to her for one thing. Now I'd got it she got me back with stories about all the boys she went with. We lay there not talking or touching each other anymore. After a little while longer she got up and dressed. I watched her and then I pulled on a pair of jeans and a T-shirt and we went back to the Wagon. Dawn told me to grab a jean jacket for the beach after so I did.

DAWN AND I walked back to the Wagon west along the seafront. She kept a space between us mostly but sometimes she came up close and bumped against me and went away again. The seafront was bright with lamplight, with the lights of the Pier up ahead, and with strings of little fairy lights suspended between the high lamp posts like sequins against the black dress of the sky. The lacquered Victorian posts were shaped with sea dragons wrapped around them and the dragons held the pearly lamps in taloned scaly paws. Moths and small bats flew against the bright lamps and in and out of the sharp toothed mouths of the bearded long-snouted sea dragons, forever frozen open in the light.

On the town side of the road were all the white hotels. Me and Steve Tardelli had worked summer jobs washing up in some of these places but I had never been through the front door of any of them. They had men out front in uniform to stop you going in unless you looked like you could afford what was inside. The hotels were more expensive the further west you went. Taylor Beaumont had worked in the kitchens at the Grand Hotel and he told us horror stories about what got put into the food there, spit and piss and stuff. The Grand was right up past the Wish Tower and into Uptown more or less. Me and Scott and Neal had cycled past it when we went up onto Beachy Head. Behind the high wall in front the large car park, on either side of the half-circle shaped driveway that swept up to the entrance of the hotel and away again, was full of big cars shining in the sun. The hotel was blazing white. Scott and Neal started jumping in the flowerbeds in the car park and two men in shiny uniforms chased them out. We laughed and swore at the men and then forgot all about it. Hotels like the Grand had nothing to do with my life.

Between the hotels and the beach there was the coast road and a series of carpet gardens. The air was thick with salt folded in with chalk from the downs and the

smell of wallflowers and roses from the gardens. We
could hear fairground music coming from the Pier.
Tourists were out walking in the warm night. Two old
Teds out for a stroll in plush drapes and winklepickers
gave Dawn hard looks. When they came close I saw that
one of the Teds had blue tattooed hands. The Teds'
greased up hair shone under the lights. I thought about
my friend Taylor Beaumont. I hoped I'd see him and
Steve Tardelli later. Maybe then I'd be able to breathe
out and be free and be myself. I didn't really know why I
was going back to the Wagon at all except that it had to
do with Dawn and Scott and this new skinhead thing
and what was going to happen next. It was like opening
a book halfway in and having to read the story through
to the end. I guess it was like Scott when he jumped off
the Pier. Once you started you couldn't stop.

A red faced out-of-towner wearing a new bright
short sleeve-shirt with flowers on it walked along eating
chips under the bright lights. Two black headed gulls
followed him and dived for the chips he dropped. A fat
woman eating a big green ice-cream and wearing a
paper hat and too tight yellow shorts stared at Dawn
and Dawn stared back until the fat woman looked away.
Dawn walked with her boots pointed outwards and her
hands in her pockets staring hard at everybody that
looked at her. A soft offshore breeze moved the fair
fringe of her feather cut and I could smell the vanilla in
her hair. I heard a little boy asking if Dawn was a boy or
a girl. I was high now and I was floating right along like
the red undersided clouds shaped like carracks and
schooners and little tenders in the sky above. Ahead of
us the minareted Pier floated above the sea on a hem of
golden lights, a dreamed spaceship in real time. On the
beach below the Pier I knew there would be local kids
kissing and feeling up kids from out of town.

We came up to the bright Pier lights and the
fairground music and the noise of a tattoo machine and
one-armed bandits and the thick smells of candy floss
and burgers. Me and Dawn used to play day long games

of air hockey on the Pier. We stood under the entrance in the summer crowds on the boardwalk. Tan long-haired skater kids wearing long cut-offs and black and white bumper boots rumbled by.

We crossed the coast road and walked into town with the Pier and the sea at our backs. In the lighted window of Fusciardi's ice-cream parlour on the corner, fifty yards from the Painted Wagon, I saw two Persian boys in soft jumpers talking with their heads close together. One of them looked at me and said something to his mate. Dawn didn't see them and I didn't say anything. Dawn ran ahead of me and spun around and gave me two fingers before running into the Wagon.

I walked into a blast of heat and noise. Eddie Beer was in there with his tattooed face. The skinheads were hot and drunk and getting up on sulphate and looking for a fight. Everybody seemed to be shouting except for Eddie. He was standing alone by the pool table in the smoke and noise. He was wearing a dirty, too big black Harrington that someone had given him. He was watching the Angelino brothers play pool and hoping that Tony or Gary would give him a shot.

Eddie Beer was seventeen or so and he was thin and shaky like a scared and beaten dog that was ready to go wild. He had bitten yellow fingers and sharp and broken yellow teeth. His head was shaved right down, not cropped, and on his head there were little red bumps and nicks where he had cut himself. Eddie was in and out of detention centres for thieving, and behind his left ear and running down his neck and under his dirty T-shirt his skin was hard and bubbly and looked like plastic where somebody had jugged him with sugar and boiling water. He drew pictures of horses. He had an India ink swastika tattooed between his eyes and India ink lightning bolts tattooed on his cheeks and he had FTW tattooed inside his lower lip. He was wearing greasy looking Falmers and steel toecaps and nobody was talking to him. I'd heard he had left home. I don't know where he slept at night but I'd guess the beach mostly.

We'd sort of been friends for a long time. Mostly when we were younger we'd stuck to being together, but when I'd started going around with Steve Tardelli and later Taylor Beaumont I'd pretty much dropped him. So whenever I saw him I felt bad. This was around the time we were eleven or twelve. Before he started tattooing himself and getting into real trouble, and long before Gary Ladd got me to kick Eddie in the head under the Pier lights. He was an ordinary looking kid then, just a bit dirty sometimes. Mostly Eddie was unhappy. People think boys like us choose trouble because we like it but anybody could see Eddie just wanted somebody to notice him and help him. His Dad was a piss artist who beat him up more or less constantly and I know that when he was younger Eddie used to make up all kinds of stories to explain the bruises he had or why he was cut up. He got himself expelled from school so he wouldn't have to keep explaining why he was always black and blue. Eddie's Mum was no use. I used to wish that my Mum would take Eddie in the way Steve Tardelli's Mum used to let me stay over. Mum just had too much to do looking after me and Scott to look after Eddie as well.

Eddie wanted to be a skinhead and he was doing what he could to get in with Scott and Bombhead. He cut his long greasy hair himself and kept it shaved down with safety razors. He couldn't keep it neat and his head was always covered with red nicks and bloody scabs. He hand pushed the tattoos on himself. If you asked me I'd say that he put the swastika on after spending time with Al Babe who most likely put Eddie up to it. Years later Steve Tardelli told me that the swastika is a sacred Hindu symbol and that the word means 'let good prevail.' Steve said that there would be good karma working in the swastika even if you wore it for the wrong reasons but that it would struggle to be felt against the bad intentions Eddie most likely had when he put it on. Steve said that if I put a swastika on me now, knowing what it meant, then it would be a powerful charm. I don't know whose idea the lightning bolts were but if it was supposed to stand for *SS* like Bombhead said then that might have been Al Babe too. *Fuck The World* was how Eddie made out he felt about everything.

Eddie always hated the Persians, even when we were little. He hated anybody who had anything nice. He couldn't speak in clear sentences about them. I do know that one time that summer Eddie had punched himself in the face or smashed his face against a wall and told Scott that he'd been fighting with the Persians in the Ocean Wave. Eddie was lonely and crazy enough to be up in the Ocean Wave by himself for sure but I believed the story I heard afterwards. I knew that story was true because Scott had told me and Scott never told lies about anything. Besides, it made perfect sense to me that someone would punch himself in the face to look good for Scott.

Eddie Beer came to the Painted Wagon every night. Without the skinheads Eddie was on his own with his drawings of horses. Scott and Bombhead let him stay. They might throw lighted cigarettes at him sometimes or punch him in the stomach or kick him in the head, but they let him stay because they recognised him as a broken soldier in the war they were fighting. Al Babe said that Eddie hated himself because he had no pride. Al Babe said Eddie was what would happen to us if we didn't stand up like white men. Bombhead said you're talking shit Al Babe. Scott said well maybe so Bomb, but if you're talking to three men you need to make sure you see four. You're telling me? Bombhead said.

Where did the skinheads come from? First you have to go inland to London and back a few years to the mods. The mods had that sharp expensive look. Italian suits and shoes but Ben Sherman shirts and Fred Perrys too. Harrington jackets. It was a look you needed money for, to keep up. It was always changing. The first skinheads were poor white kids who wanted to look good but who couldn't keep up with the mod look. The mods had a bit more money. They worked in the city as office boys and messengers. The mods were looking up and out. The skinheads worked as labourers, scaffolders, and dockers. The same jobs their fathers and brothers did.

The skinheads stripped the mod look down to workboots, straight-leg jeans, and braces. Look like what you are but put an edge to it. Sta-Prest, Ben Sherman shirts, Fred Perrys, Crombie coat or a sheepskin maybe in the winter. Heads cropped down to a number three or maybe a two but no shorter, sideburns. They were called hard mods at first, then skinheads. The first skinheads lived and worked and partied with Jamaican boys their own age. London born but strong on Jamaica. Rude boys. The skins borrowed the styles. The Rude boys had ska and rock steady, bluebeat, sounds like Alton Ellis, Laurel Aitken. Desmond Dekker, Dandy Livingstone. Prince Buster of course. The white kids and the black kids loved the sounds. What it was, when you think about it, was poor white and black kids getting together and making something of their own. There was that pride to it and saying no to being invisible. Maybe you didn't know about that. A lot of people think that all skinheads are Nazis. That's what the word means to them. Mostly the skinheads beat on rich kids or kids they thought were rich like the hippies, but some skins attacked Asian kids too so maybe that's where all the Nazi stuff started. Skinheads hated the hippies. Skinheads couldn't drop out. Skinheads had to work.

With our town and in my family it started with Punk. Before then, like I say, all me and Scott ever did was go to the beach. Then everything arrived all at once. Scott turning thirteen and starting to look around and weigh things. There were no Asians in our town, but there had always been Persians and they had always had money. Mum told Scott once that at first there were a couple of Persians who opened hairdressing shops when she was a little kid and it started from there. And there were the rich white kids who lived in Uptown and Paradise Woods where the public school and the golf course and the money was.

Mum worked in a supermarket and cleaned houses in Uptown to feed us and there was nothing left over. Scott started busting out and getting into fights, with rich kids mostly, which is something I only worked out later, because I wasn't conscious of there being a pattern. It takes twenty years to begin to work things out. He was on his own Scott, picking fights with somebody he didn't like the look of or who spoke funny, but it didn't seem to do him any good. Maybe it's like Ponyboy Curtis says in my book, you can't win against them no matter how hard you try.

It could get to you, the no money no Dad thing.

Then Punk happened. What was the first punk record? The way I look at it the first punk record was the first one you heard. The Damned *New Rose* then the first Clash LP. Scott was sixteen. When you take everything else away the sound of punk was the first thing that was ours. I thought Scott fell into it too hard as the answer. Like being a punk was a matter of life and death for him but really after that first three minute record, punk, for most people, was nothing more than a faked attitude. Pretty soon a lot of the rich kids we hated started getting into punk and Scott was hacked off about that. How could you be a rich punk? You could be a rich punk if punk meant nothing but a look. And Scott hated how quickly people in town started laughing at the punks. Because for some people who had nothing punk was everything.

Scott and Bombhead took it up to the next level. I don't know where they pulled the look out from but it put them both properly on the outside and I think that's why they did it. If you saw these two walking down the road in boots and braces you'd get out of the way, you wouldn't laugh at them. Scott just refused to be nobody. It burned in him. Bombhead had his own reasons for putting a wall up around himself. And after Scott and

Bombhead showed the way all these other boys found the power in boots and braces.

The rich kids couldn't fake the skinhead look and what the skinheads stood for. Kids with money don't understand what a gang is for. You might see a bunch of bikers beating on a skinhead and you'd help him even if you got a kicking yourself because there was nobody else to help us and skinhead was your family.

The skinheads were telling the rich kids and the Persians Uptown to fuck off. This was our town. Punk was nothing compared. Punk was just fashion. I mean you could be a weekend punk. Leave the house normal and spike your hair with grease from a bag of chips on your way into town. You're wearing a ratty pair of deck shoes and drainpipe jeans. Under your jean jacket you can hide a ripped up T-shirt. You couldn't do that if you were a skinhead and that's what Scott and Bombhead were showing and telling people those summer nights in the Wagon. Being a skinhead was a way of life.

THE WAGON was packed to the door. Scott saw me and
he pointed to the bar and made the talking sign with his
hand. Scott's white button down was wet in places and
sticking to him. Bombhead was up close and talking to
Scott.

Dawn was play fighting with Gary Angelino after
jumping on him first thing in the door. I say play
fighting but Dawn never held back on her punches and
Gary had to keep her off by wrestling her. They had
cleared a space and skinheads were cheering them on
and lobbing beer at them.

I pushed my way up to the bar and got a few hard
slaps on the back. Julie Spanish pulled me close and
kissed me. She said hello Kimmy, we missed you. Julie
had a husky voice that always set sparks off inside me.
She was tan with a just off the beach red blush on her
skin. I could smell Ambre Solaire on her. Julie always
looked sleepy. Her black eyes were half closed and her
lips were full and red. Her hand was soft and cool on the
back of my neck. She gave me two cans of Breaker for
free.

I was staring at Julie like a dope when Scott grabbed
me from behind and picked me up and swung me round
fierce. I told you he was strong. I tried to break his hold
on me but I couldn't. I could feel his wet shirt against my
back. He put me down hard and I turned to look at him.
Scott was grinning fit to burst. Bombhead was smiling.

"Get us some rum!" Scott shouted at Julie.

Julie put some ice in plastic half-pint cups and free
poured Captain Morgan's rum into the cups until they
were full.

Scott grinned at me again and said, "Fuck me Horse,
she's trying to kill us." He drank off half his rum
straightaway and leaned over the bar and kissed Julie on
the mouth. Everybody was watching them and Scott
knew they were. He was all flushed up and he was
drunk and sweating but his clear gold eyes on me told

88

me he knew what he was about. He put Julie down and stood in front of me with his boots planted on the ground.

"You look like she came across," Scott said.

"And I still got my hair." I was drunk.

Scott laughed. "Are you two back together then?"

"Why?"

"Cos Bombhead's been keeping an eye out for her but now you're back he can let up."

I looked at Bombhead. "Why do you need to keep an eye on her. What's she done?"

Bombhead said, "Dug doesn't like it she's a skinhead is what we heard. It makes Hazim nervous, like Dug's too much on our side. That's the last thing Dug is though. He's got the hump all round because the Persians are asking questions but what Dug's really worried about is that Dawn will tell us something she shouldn't."

"Like what?"

Scott drank off the rest of his rum. The cans of Breaker Julie had given me were sweating on the bar and Scott took one and opened it and drank. He leaned back against the bar with his arms spread and looked at me hard. Bombhead took a step to me and started talking quietly.

"We know he's been doing it forever but where's the law says Dug has to run all the drugs? He sits up in that garage eating downers and listening to all that Hawkwind bollocks and thinking no-one can touch him. Maybe Dawn will tell us something that will give us an edge. That's what he's been worrying about ever since you two got together. That's why you got sent away I reckon. At first I thought that was why she became a skinhead."

"Has she said anything?"

"She won't say anything about him, not to us," Bombhead said. "You being back puts Hazim under more pressure. The Persians will think everything's loaded up on our side. Maybe Hazim already thinks we're getting better rates. He'll think we're getting the shit for nothing if he puts you and Dawn together. And Dug's going to freak because he'll think she's talking to you and you're talking to me."

"You really think so?" I said to Scott.

"Mate that's why he went to all that trouble before to drop you in it," Scott said, "I thought you'd have sorted that out by now. What were you doing up there?"

"Why doesn't Dug just tell Hazim the truth?"

"Nobody tells the truth round this kind of thing Kim," Bombhead said. "Everybody bullshits everybody else. Besides, Dug knows it would make him look weak in front of them if he said anything. He'll think it's best to carry on like nothing's changed which it hasn't. Everybody's paying the same, except the Persians don't know that. What's going to be stoking up his paranoia is the connections he'll be making between you and Dawn and your brother."

"So what do you want me to do?"

Scott took another big slug of beer. The rum in the plastic cup was getting warm in my hand.

"You need to be careful," he said. "When you're out with her watch out the Persians don't jump you. They might try and get to Dug through her. And don't be going near Dug's garage. Don't be walking around places late with Dawn where Dug can pick you off. He's going to know you're home and seeing her and that's going to burn him so keep out of his way. He's a fucking looper, so stay close to home. To me and Bomb."

Bombhead and Scott looked at each other.

"What?" I said.

Scott said, "I need you to talk to her, and we want to hear anything you can find out."

"Come on Scott I'm not doing that. She doesn't tell me anything anyway."

"Look mate I know what it sounds like. I need to find out who his suppliers are. He keeps all that super quiet. I know people who can get me bits and bobs but nothing like the weight Dug gets. I want to cut him out. Dug makes money on the mark up and we're losing out and he keeps us on a string. Hazim too but fuck him. He's in this for the laugh, he doesn't need the money. But we do and we're not making enough to get away with so we got to step it up or we'll be fucking stuck here forever. The first man who gets to those suppliers and cuts out Dug wins. So keep your ears open and see what you can find out. That's all I'm saying Kim, mostly just look after yourself but if you hear anything tell me."

"What's happened to you Scott?"

Anger flared across my brother's face like a shooting star. His gold eyes flashed. Bombhead kind of dropped back and there was just me and Scott. He was panting hot. His hair was the colour of wet sand.

"Stop fucking daydreaming Kim. This is what's happening now. You think I want to be a roofer all my life? Get your head out of the clouds. What do you think there's going to be for you in this town after the summer ends? This is what's really going on. This is the way out."

Scott reached into his jeans pocket and took out some more money and held it out to me like he was showing it to me.

"There's proper money in this Kim. You always said you wanted to be in on stuff with me, here's your chance."

I took the money and looked at it. I loved Scott. He was everything to me. I stuffed the money in my pocket.

"There were two Persians outside on the corner when I came in."

"Did they see you?" Scott said.

I nodded. Bombhead ghosted away.

"What do you reckon?"

"Could be anything or nothing," Scott said. Bombhead was back.

"Anything?"

"No mate," said Bombhead, "Not a sign. What do you want to do?"

Scott looked around the Wagon.

"Give the boys a run out I reckon. Put in a few windows at the Ocean Wave. If Hazim did send those two he'll know we know. Round everybody up at closing Bomb, let them know what's going on."

In Scott's wild heart and pride he was connected all the way back to 1969 and the days of skinhead glory, and sometimes I thought he'd taken it on himself to try and make something out of all of us. With me I think it was on him all the time, what was going to become of me. When Scott talked about getting out and going away it was the first time I realised he wouldn't be a skinhead forever. And I think Scott wanted to be a proud skinhead because he wanted people to talk about him when he was gone.

Dawn was sitting and talking to Eddie Beer. They were sitting on two backless stools and Eddie had his head on her shoulder and Dawn was stroking him and talking to him. Not when we were little but later there were always stories that Eddie was being fucked by his Dad but like Taylor Beaumont says, maybe because we didn't have Dads we were always open to believe stories like that. Eddie was out where the buses don't run, Taylor said, but he wasn't the only one. We were all in Borneo together five years ago travelling up the Skrang river, Steve, Taylor, and me, and Taylor asked me if I had ever noticed how many boys we knew in our town who had been sent away and I said, yes mate, of course.

I've said how boys I knew were sent to special schools, it wasn't just me, or to detention centres and borstals, like Bombhead and Gary Ladd. Al Babe as well, I found out later. Like Bombhead, Taylor's brother Ted had been in Send. And there were also boys like Joe Winterland who was sent to a monastery near Lewes for three years for burning down his house because, he said, his heart was on fire. High in the Wagon it came to me that Dawn and Eddie Beer were the only people I knew who had Dads.

Skinheads were getting in two cans at a time and speed drinking as Julie tried to close up. I went into the

toilet. The walls in there were painted black and the
skinheads had used anything with a sharp edge to write
on the walls. On the wall at head height where you
stood and pissed Dawn had cut in a big jagged D A W N
with little eight hole bovver boots on the feet of the A.
Somebody had scratched two horizontal lines coming
out of the second upright on the N. There was BHA
written up there, and FUCK OFF PALACE, KILL ALL
PERSIANS, and SKINS with the S's stretched out and
sharp so that they looked like the lightning bolts
tattooed on Eddie Beer's face. Somebody had written
EDDIE IS A STUPID CUNT – OI! YOU'RE A STUPID
CUNT EDDIE.

When I came out I went over to Dawn. Eddie Beer sat
up straight and stared at me. He was short-sighted but
he would never wear glasses, and he looked at me like
he couldn't decide if he knew me or if I was someone
who shouldn't be in there. When he was little nobody
was going to take him to get a pair of glasses. I guess he
was on something too, he always was. Eddie kind of
leaned in to look at me. Then he recognised me and
smiled and showed his broken teeth and said, "Mate,
Kim mate, you all right? Where you been?"

I stared at the tattoos on his face. The swastika and
the lightning bolts seemed to come off his face and float
in front of my eyes. I wondered if he remembered me
kicking him in the head the last time Gary Ladd got
home. I was trying to make sense of what Scott had
asked me to do. Still there was the money in my pocket.
I wasn't thinking about Eddie Beer who looked happy
now. One summer I spent every day with him but I
couldn't remember the last time I'd spoken to him.

"We're going to the Ocean Wave Kim. Me and your
brother and everybody. You're coming aren't you
Dawn?"

"Fuck off Eddie," I said.

Dawn made a little barking sound like the sound you
make when you hit someone and gave me a look that
went straight into me.

"What," she said to me, "you a tough nut now like Scott? You can show me how tough you are when we get up there, you want to."

I reached out for my can and knocked it over, spilling beer over the mess on the table. Maybe I thought Eddie was the only person in the Wagon who wasn't tougher than me. If I did think that I was wrong. Maybe it was the way Eddie put his need out there. Eddie didn't seem to notice what I'd said but I could feel Dawn close down against me. I didn't want to go to the Ocean Wave and at the same time I did. I worried that if I had to fight somebody I wouldn't be able to but I was locked into going.

Scott was behind the bar and started loading up little skinheads with slabs of Breaker to take to the beach for afterwards. Al Babe was sitting on a corner banquette with three girls who'd come in late looking to buy some Rocky. Al Babe had a cigarette stuck in the corner of his mouth and he was sitting with his legs spread wide so the girls were all kind of crushed into the corner of the seat near the wall. Al Babe's Levi's were tight against his cock and balls and stopped at the top of his high shined blood red boots. One girl was Galley Mouratidis but I didn't know the others except that one of them was called Cloud. Galley was wearing hip high, frayed cut-offs and a tight, sky blue Fruit of the Loom T-shirt over a black bikini top. Galley was tall with dirty blonde hair and thick dark eyebrows. She had long brown legs and sitting on the low banquette her legs were stretched out awkwardly in front of her like a young deer that hasn't learnt to stand. She was sixteen and she had a broken nose and a dirty laugh. Al Babe was leaning in and talking to Galley and I couldn't hear what he was saying but when we left the pub the girls were with him. I was scared to leave and go outside but I followed Al Babe, Galley, Cloud and the other girl out into the still warm night.

Scott stood in the light of the electric Breaker sign shining in the window of the Painted Wagon. He was sweating and stamping his feet.

Scott looked at me and said, "Don't look so worried Horse. It's just a bit of fun. You used to be up for a laugh, what happened to you up there?"

"Nothing," I said, "Come on, let's go."

Going down to the beach and heading west to the Ocean Wave we danced on the tops of cars and roared at the sky. Bombhead jumped in a flying drop-kick onto Tony Angelino. Scott got in a horse bite on Bomb as he lay in the road fighting with Tony. A little gang of skaters off the seafront saw us coming and got out of our way. Gary Angelino had his board with him and a couple of the skaters nodded at him going by and one long-haired blond kid called his name. Gary looked straight ahead and said nothing to the skaters and Scott gave him the kind of look he used to give me when I'd surprised him and done something right. I could see Gary trying not to smile with it.

Scott put himself in front and we all fanned out behind him, Bombhead on the right and Tony Angelino on the left, Al Babe with his arm around Galley Mouratidis and her two mates walking arm in arm and giggling. Al Babe carried a white towel under the arm that wasn't around Galley. Julie walked just behind Scott and kind of hooked the fingers of her right hand in the tight back pocket of his Levi's. Scott was looking left and right. There were a whole bunch of little skinheads following on behind Gary Angelino the way kids follow a boy who is going to fight, close by and excited but leaving a space around Gary for him to walk in. I got some sea air in me and my thoughts came too fast to catch. Eddie Beer was close to me and his mouth was open and his red tongue was hanging out past his pointed yellow teeth.

There was no wind and the tide was way out so that the water was hard to hear but you could if you wanted to, and if you really listened. I stopped hearing it. My eyes were on Scott and the skinheads. Boots and heads were lit up by the lights along the front, the hard head of

a boy or a panther tattoo flaring as the skinheads passed
under the sea dragon lamps. My skin was like fire and I
was hot inside. It was like I had a fever but I guess I was
just high and drunk. Up ahead a family group of out-of-
towners coming back late to their hotel jumped like
rabbits when they heard us coming and I was glad. They
ran inside. This was better than where I'd been. Fuck
that place. I could feel my heart thumping and the blood
beat in my ears. Scott turned round and looked at me
and asked me a question with his flashing gold eyes and
I said yes.

THE SOUTHERN stars were out and I could smell
honeysuckle. Scott had us move Indian file in the
shadows under the horse chestnut trees on the avenue
that approached the western side of the Ocean Wave.
Away from the seafront the streets were darker. None of
us belonged this far Uptown, and we did not need Scott
to tell us to stay quiet or to keep away from the alarms
that would come on if we passed too close to the tall,
closed gates of the big houses and bring the police we
never saw in our part of town down upon us.

The Ocean Wave was a two-floor L-shaped pub at the
corner of two wide tree-lined avenues. Kelly had taken
me there once. I remember she seemed to know
everybody in there. There were big picture windows
that opened onto wrought iron ornamental balconies on
the upstairs floor and you could just see the sea and part
of the Wish Tower from the east facing balcony. From
the west facing balcony you could watch the sun fall
over Paradise Woods. There was a long-wave surfboard
with the name of the pub painted on it hanging from a
salt rusted bracket and chains screwed high up on the
east facing wall. White and pink honeysuckle spilled
down the red brick walls.

Two men stood on the west facing balcony. They
were black shapes against the sky that was made violet
by the moon and the stars, not people at all. They stood
close together and I thought I could hear them talking.
We watched other people leave the pub and just ahead
of us, crouched down by a mud-splashed, barley
Mercedes, Scott held his arm straight out from his side to
tell us he was waiting for the two men we had seen
upstairs. They came out. Lights were turned off behind
them so that when they stood out front it was dark. One
of the men stopped to light a cigarette and the flame
from the lighter lit up the man's face and his rings and
the thick gold necklace he was wearing and now you

could see he was a Persian.

I rushed shouting with Gary and Eddie and the little skinheads from under the horse chestnut trees towards the men and a full beer can was thrown from behind me and hit the man with the lighter on the side of the head and he went down on one knee. We were on him straight away like dogs. The other man ran away and we let him go. We punched and kicked the man who was down. The man lay on the ground shouting words in a language none of us understood but that I would hear, years later, in other countries. The smell of his blood folded in with honeysuckle. He was on the ground with his knees drawn up to his stomach and his arms tight around his head. We tried to pull his arms away from his head to hit him better. I looked back and saw Scott and Bombhead and Tony Angelino and Al Babe watching us from under the horse chestnut trees. The stars flashed in Scott's golden eyes.

There were all these fires inside and I was trying to punch the man on the ground. I couldn't kick him because I was wearing flip-flops. I don't know if I hit him but I wanted to. I won't lie about that. There were boots going in again and again. I heard myself shouting something. The lights in the Ocean Wave came on. The man on the ground had blood all over his face and in his light beard and in the black curls of his hair. I saw Eddie Beer's dirty yellow hand reach out and rip the bright gold necklace from the man's neck. I could hear Galley Mouratidis screaming and I could hear sirens. Scott shouted at us to get out and then we were all running. I couldn't see Dawn anywhere. I took off my flip-flops and carried them and ran in bare feet along the clean and well kept avenues down to the sea.

At the beach I ran to the water. The tide had turned and was not so far out. I ran to the edge of the beach stones and took off my jean-jacket and jeans and T-shirt and dropped them on the beach with my flip-flops. I ran over the cool inky wet sand and into the sea until the black water was hip high and then I dived full length in and under and then I was up and swimming fast. Some of the skinheads followed me but I couldn't tell who. I was a great swimmer. I used to wonder sometimes if I was the best swimmer in the town. I had dreams of swimming against some rich and popular boy and beating him in front of everybody and being a hero. I loved how I looked in the water. I stopped and swam again and then stopped and floated. I closed my eyes and I could see the man on the ground. I could see blood on the gold necklace and hear Galley screaming.

The moon seemed big and too close. The salt water pushed me up towards it. I pushed my hair out of my eyes and righted myself in the water and looked back to the beach. Floating in water that was lit by the moon and stars I watched as Dawn stripped down to her black knickers and folded her arms across her chest. I swam a lazy crawl in towards her. She walked dreamily in to the sea with the water hushing up around her waist as more skinhead boys ran past her howling, not wanting to swim but not wanting to be shit-outs. If you didn't swim you'd hear about it later from the boys who did.

Bombhead splashed Dawn and Dawn, turning to see him bent in the surf with his hands cupping water again, let her arms fall to her sides and stuck herself out and Bombhead fell back splash in the surf like someone had hit him. Dawn started to laugh and looked out to sea and maybe saw me and turned and ran back up the beach, small and pale as thrown away paper and somehow faraway up on the dark beach. For just a moment in the dark her body seemed somehow split and separated by her black knickers.

I caught a wave and raced in on it with a high sweeping arm stroke and stood when it was too shallow to swim. I ran past Bombhead after Dawn, running with my legs high, trying to run over the water and not through it, my heart sounding loud inside my head. I grabbed my jeans off the beach and put them on and ran up the beach. I wanted to be with her and I didn't want to be with anybody else. When I caught up to her she was getting dressed in a shelter on the front. She was still wet when she put on her jeans and Fred Perry and boots. Skaters had tagged the shelter. The forever repeated sound of the sea was kind of softened down and muted in there. I was wet and cold in just my jeans. My hair was long and wet and cold against my back.

She wouldn't let me hug her or kiss her on the throat or anything. I put my hand flat on her crop and pushed it down and let go and the short wet hair sprang back up and my hand was wet and I could smell vanilla on the night air.

"What's the matter?"

"Stop playing with my fucking hair Kim."

I didn't know what I'd done wrong. I thought she'd be pleased with me. She had goose bumps on her arms and she shivered and she wouldn't look at me.

"Come back to the house," I said, "I'll sneak you in."

"I'm going home Kim."

"What for? Come back with me."

She put her little hands on my chest and pushed me away as hard as she could.

"Listen," she said, "just fuck off and leave me alone."

I must have been looking at her all dumb faced because she said, "There was just one of them Kim."

When I still didn't say anything she said, "Don't be like them Kim. It won't make whatever's bugging you any better. Tough isn't doing everything Scott and Bombhead say. I know I tease you but I like you because you're different to them. Don't you get it?"

She stood on the toes of her boots and gave me a kiss on the cheek.

"I'll see you later," she said. "Don't look at me like that, just think about what I said."

"Do you want me to get Bombhead?"

"What for?"

"To walk you home."

"Who have you been talking to?"

When I didn't say anything she laughed and said, "Tell Scott I can get home by myself."

She walked out of the shelter and away. I knew better than to try and stop her. I'd never been able to stop her doing anything she wanted to do.

On the beach the Angelinos started a fire where the old one had burned down. Gary went around the beach in the dark finding stuff to burn. Tony had a small yellow can of lighter fuel in his Harrington pocket and he squirted some on the little flames his brother got started and the fire roared up and caught and held. Gary carried driftwood along the beach to the fire and Eddie Beer would have thrown it all on at once if Tony hadn't shouted at him. We all stood by the fire to get dry. The ranking skins and me stood closest to the fire. All of us except Al Babe in jeans and bare-chested. Al Babe stood next to Tony Angelino.

"You know who that was don't you Scott?" Al Babe said.

"Who would you say it was Al?" my brother said.

"It was Ahmed wasn't it Al?" Tony Angelino said.

"I thought it was," Al Babe said, "It looked like him. What d'you reckon Scott?"

"I'd say so," Scott said. He smiled. "You did all right there boys."

"What do you think Hazim will do when he hears we got his mate?"Al Babe said.

"I don't know and I don't give a fuck," Scott said, "I guess we'll find out soon enough. I doubt they'll hit us front on though, that's not his style. So I reckon we're safe here. I don't think Hazim's ever been east of the Pier. He'll have to do something though so be careful where you go on your own, all right Kim?"

You might not think so but for just that little while I felt okay. Maybe I was even happy a little bit that Dawn had cunted me off. She had said that she liked me and I had not heard her say anything like that to me for a long time, so I quickly forgot the other things she said. I stood between Scott and Bombhead. Scott put his warm big hand on my bare shoulder. He wasn't looking at me but it didn't matter. I thought that if I got the chance I would do what he asked me. I could be tough like my brother. It's not so often that you feel like you belong somewhere. I looked across the fire at Eddie Beer who was looking blissed out. For the first time I got how strong you might feel if you were a skinhead. That night I believed that the skinheads would never leave a man behind to get a kicking.

I reached up and pulled my hair over my shoulder and squeezed it until the sea water fell from the ends. I held my hair out in front of me to see how long it was and I saw Bombhead looking at me with a flat and dead serious expression that did not change when I caught him looking.

Al Babe pushed out the message about the Kingdom of Sussex. He talked softly about the white girls the Persians were supposed to keep in Uptown. Girls we knew who were knocked out by the money the Persians had, by all the gold and perfume, the free hash and downers. Al Babe said the girls would be taken back to some flat in Uptown and gang-banged blind while a bunch of dirty Persians filmed them. He had stories about white girls being dumped up in Paradise Woods above Uptown. Al Babe talked to us, sitting on the dark beach in the warm night with the stars high overhead and the sea violet and uncontained. He said that we had to hold the little ground we had left and fight to take back the ground we'd lost, and our faces became hot with more than the beach fire. Everybody wants to belong to something I guess. To a tribe. Everybody else did, it seemed like, so why not people like us?

Al Babe had his towel round his waist and he was stroking his tan, flat belly and the girls were sitting at his feet. Blonde, tall Galley Mouratidis had her hand on the backs of his legs and her hand was reaching up under the towel. Cloud, her sunburnt skin glowing against her snowy white halter top and high cut white shorts, was skinning up and when she finished she lit the joint and passed it up to Al Babe. Al smoked the joint and smiled. Tony Angelino was looking at Al and then Tony looked

at Scott. Scott shook his head and started laughing and
Tony cracked up. Al Babe was smoking Rocky and
getting his arse felt and looking at Scott and Tony and
the rest of us laughing at him and Al was saying "What?
What?"

Julie put her arms around Scott.

"Fucking Al Babe man," Tony was coughing and
laughing at the same time, "you look like a dog with two
cocks."

Bombhead had the sounds down low, so all you
could hear was this soft offbeat Ka-*chinnk*...Ka-
chinnk...Ka-*chinnk* floating in the night. We all had beer
and there was some Thunderbird and some Rocky going
around and we settled down to the buzz and watched
little orange wood sparks rise and slowly float away like
stars burning out in the warm dark air. We watched the
low gentle black surf come in and out, kind of hushed
sounding like the low playing King Tubby sounds from
Bombhead's beat box. If you looked at the Pier lights
they got all blurry and it was hard to stop looking at
them. I could never look at light reflected on the water
without thinking that the lights were coming from under
the sea. In my head there were lighted watermen
swimming up from the bottom of the sea to take me
home. Bombhead turned the sounds up to a kicking tune
that was driven by tom toms and choppy guitars with a
wild flute riding over the top.

"King Tubby," Bombhead said, "*Fugitive Dub*.
Sounds of the summer."

"Turn it up loud Bomb," Scott called, and Bombhead
turned up the mix so we could all hear the fast rumbling
tune echoing over the beach. I was high and the thick
drums got inside me but not in the spacey way the Pier
lights and the sound of the sea did. This was a tune that
made you want to dance or fight and I got up and
danced all crazy around the fire. The heat of the fire and
the music seemed somehow connected and blazed in me
and licked up my insides. The voice in my head that was
always there and talking and telling me how I was

nothing and how I was shit was gone, and because it was never gone I let it go and whirled and kicked up sand and jumped around the fire to stop it from coming back. All the faces of the skinheads were lit up by firelight and they were laughing as they watched me dance, Scott and Bombhead and everybody.

Then Bombhead turned the sounds off and things quietened down again and I was left alone. I had a joint in my hand that had gone out and I lit it and smoked. Scott was sitting up with Julie backed into him. He had his arms around her and was holding her tight and talking softly to her with his mouth close to her ear. He looked over at me and smiled and gave me a thumb up, then a thumb down. I gave him a thumb up back and wiggled my thumb and little finger in a surfer's wave and he smiled. Then he cuddled into Julie again and rested his head on her back. After a little while he moved and spoke to Julie again and they lay down together by the fire, their arms around each other, and Tony Angelino walked over and put his Harrington over them and Scott smiled up at him and then they were still. Tony walked away up the beach to the road with his back turned to us and with his right fist raised. Bombhead got up and saw me looking at my brother and Julie and gave me a low whistle and waved at me and said "Good to see you Kimmy," and looked at me hard and walked away from the beach.

Eddie Beer had crashed. He was jerking and talking in his sleep, and the lightning bolts tattooed on his face kind of jumped in time. Al Babe was off down the beach somewhere with Galley Mouratidis. I didn't know where Cloud and her mate were. Maybe they were all down there with Al Babe. There was a little bit of beer left in the can I had and I drank that and finished the joint and got up and walked west along the beach. I heard what Scott had said but I didn't want to stay on the beach without Dawn and I didn't want to go home. I knew that all the strong feelings I had for me would be gone when I woke up in the morning.

"**SOUNDS TO** me like your brother's putting you out where you're going to get hurt," Steve Tardelli said. "Like he's using you."

"Maybe he wants to toughen me up."

"You aren't cut out to be a tough nut Kimmy," Steve said, "Don't you know that? And why would you want to be?"

We were talking up on the Wish Tower lawns. It was late and there was nobody around but me and Steve and Taylor and thousands of distant stars in the violet sky above. I could see no lights shining in the windows of the white hotels. I had written to Steve to tell him that my first night home I would be at the Wish Tower and he and Taylor had waited up for me all this time. Steve was wearing Levi's and black Chukka shoes and a windcheater with a book sticking out of the pocket.

Steve Tardelli had big ears and big ideas. His nose was long and very straight and he had fair hair that he kept cut short at the back and the sides and that he let grow in thick curls in front that never seemed to get wet when it rained or when he swam. His blue eyes were clear like water in a still pond. Steve was away off into himself a lot of the time, he seemed kind of gravely cool and somewhere else in those days, but he was quick to smile and laugh. He had a thin, down turned mouth that with his hatchet nose made him seem less open than he was. I say that like I'm talking about somebody I used to know, maybe somebody who's gone, but he's still the same pretty much, still slim and boyish in Levi's and white T-shirt and full sleeves of rocks and flowers and falling water and whirlwinds at the elbows. That's what Steve does now, he puts tattoos on people. I've got some handpushed work on me from when I was out in Asia one time but otherwise Steve's put all my work on me.

By a small tower of beer cans Taylor Beaumont lay on the grass star shaped, flat on his back with a busted up straw hat over his face. He was wearing a red and black check shirt, Comfort shoes and old Levi's.

"There's an elephant sitting on me," Taylor said.

The lawns were between the sea and the road going away up to the downs in the west. The Wish Tower was one of a series of round Martello towers built to defend the south coast during the Napoleonic Wars. It stood overlooking the sea at the top of a small hill that rose from the green lawns. Above the old fort, in the sky that was splashed with stars, the moon was some other bright land shining on the sea. It wouldn't be long before the sky began to lighten and the sun to rise.

"A hippo," Taylor said.

What was Steve Tardelli to me? He was the first person who listened to what I had to say. Without ever saying so Steve and Taylor and a handful of other boys lay claim to being different. Every town has them, the boys who seem to come from outer space. Steve was a source, the one who turned the light on in my house.

Steve's mum worked in a bakery in the town, and his house was always full of gingerbread men and custard pies, éclairs and Danish pastries. There was this constant sweetness at Steve's house, or so it seems to me now. I stayed there a lot. You could look out and see the sea shining and permanent under the low summer moon. Late at night when we had come back from being out drinking beer and talking somewhere, we would lie on the floor with the windows open and drink sweet tea and skin up and we would listen to the sea, its going away and coming back. And the big thing is I could sleep there and know that whatever else happened to me in the night I wouldn't be woken up by the police banging on the door looking for Scott. I loved it there.

I stopped stealing, I think, because of Steve. There were always books in his house that I wanted to take home and he was all right with that. He was happy to share with you. Steve trusted you, that's what it was, and I hadn't had that before. He gave me books to read. *Huckleberry Finn* I remember and *Borstal Boy*, and I read them and came back to him and we talked about them. I read all the books he gave me and tried to find books he didn't know. When I gave him *The Outsiders* to read he said not to take it as the story of my life.

The thing is we were boys and we were southern boys too. Most of the boys I knew wouldn't talk about how they felt. It was like a law. Maybe when we were high in the hot night and talked about everything, all at once, and that was what getting high was for at first. Steve though, you could open your heart to him at any time and he would listen. It was dangerous to give anything of yourself away, but Steve wasn't going to laugh at you if you told him you read books. And because all the other boys you knew would give you a kicking for saying something like that, you learned to hide it and just put on the hard face. So someone like Steve, he was always going to stand out, because you could open up to him and be yourself, even if you weren't sure who that was.

"Boys," Taylor said, "Give us a hand up."

We pulled Taylor up. He pushed his straw hat back on his head and looked at me. Behind his Buddy Holly specs his eyes were a blurred green, like dirty water in a fish tank. The one condition of Taylor's affection for me was that I remain peaceful. Taylor loved to tell and hear stories about hard boys but he got spooked if you so much as raised your voice when he was nearby. When they were together, Taylor's Mum and Dad had their fights below the room where Taylor tried to sleep. His brother Ted wanted to be Gene Vincent and came on like a slouching hood from a 50s teen movie. A mugger and a sneak thief, Ted carried a switchblade, and he was locked up in Send for a mugging that summer. The principle of peacefulness Taylor lived by was difficult to hold and it was dangerous to him. To other boys it made him suspect, and you might think that Taylor's fast mouth and rockabilly style were the front he put up for protection. There is some truth in that, but when he looked at me with his sad and cloudy eyes I always thought that the boy he was turning himself into was meant to take the place of the scared fat kid in glasses he believed himself to be in his heart. When things got tough for him Taylor loved to drink. He poured it down to put out the fires inside.

Steve said, "It's good to see you Kim."

"I'm seeing two of him just now," Taylor said.

"It's like that Taylor is it?" I said.

"I don't know mate," Taylor said, "You tell me. Am I looking at my friend Kimmy who went away or some tough nut pretending to be him?"

"All right Taylor, he's only just come home," Steve said.

"I don't want to hear about skinheads Kim," Taylor said. He'd found a full beer and was drinking it. "I don't like your brother or the stormtroopers who follow him about."

"You wouldn't tell him that though, would you Taylor?"

"No Kim I wouldn't," Taylor said, "'because he'd hit me and I'm not into that either, funnily enough."

If this had been an ordinary summer I would have lived in Steve's pockets, but the second I saw Dawn with her feather cut and boots, and spoke to my brother, I was locked in with the skinheads. So my first night home was one of the few times I saw Steve and Taylor that summer. It was a small town but they were living in a different world to me, a place where they dropped California Sunshine and had water pistol fights on the Pier, and sat up all night talking about poetry or watching Tex Avery cartoons. I'd see them out sometimes but when I did it was always like I was trying to catch up with them. I'd see a flash of white T, or a square of plaid shirt and a glimpse of flat top moving on ahead. Sometimes I saw Steve out collecting on the beach in the early mornings.

Steve's been a beachcomber all his life, and when I think about my friend it's still not the tattooing I think about first, even now after all this time and everything he's put on me, but Steve on a beach in early winter wearing a windcheater, old jeans, and chukka shoes and standing on a rise of stones. The sea all choppy and alive at his back, and Steve holding driftwood pale as bone, a piece of sandglass, or a broken toy. He'd take this stuff home and arrange the different things in one of the glass-fronted boxes he'd made, and how he put the things together made a story that you could feel. All these thrown away or broken or found things; he'd make them into something beautiful. That's the thing about Steve. He makes things. I mean, you take Scott and the skinheads, and what were they making? I can see that now.

And that was Steve's thing with boys too. He picked me out of nowhere to be a friend to, and he saw connections between me and Taylor Beaumont that I didn't see and that seemed unlikely at first, but here we are all these years later.

Taylor Beaumont liked to say there was nothing to blood but I think he was wrong there. He said me and Steve were lucky not to have Dads. Later I saw that Taylor believed you could elect blood and make a good family with your friends and choose what you stood for that way. The way it happened with my daughters, well let's say I know what he means now, but back then I wasn't like Steve, who didn't have a brother, or Taylor, who thought his brother was a low life. When I was little Scott had always been there when I needed him, and while there might be a hundred things going through me when I was with him, always the strongest feeling I had was that he was my hero.

"What's in it for you?" Steve said.

"I don't know, maybe some money to get away Scott says."

"Get away where?"

"I don't know."

"You'd have to look in the mirror afterwards and it won't matter where you are."

"What do you know about Dug, Taylor?"

"Well I know he's your girlfriend's Dad, Kim," Taylor said.

"I know that Taylor, fucking hell."

"I think Taylor means you have to think about it Kim. We don't know about Dads. How that works. I mean the whole thing sounds crazy to me and I don't think you should have anything to do with it, but whatever you're thinking you have to see you can't ask her to tell on her Dad."

"What you should do," Taylor said, "is tell Dawn what Scott asked you to do."

"Maybe I'll go jump off Beachy Head while I'm at it."

I didn't say anything else. I lay on the grass listening to Taylor and Steve talk. I tried not to hear the sound of boots hitting the Persian's head but they came to me then and I couldn't block them out. On the beach Scott said to me, keep tonight to yourself Kim. Your hippy mates have got a fucked up idea about the Persians. This is our town, my brother said, not the sand niggers'. He waited to see if I was going to say anything. I didn't. What can I tell you? He was everything to me in those days. Then he said, I saw you Kimmy, you were into it. He was right. I was into it, and because I was into it I was ashamed.

Me and Taylor and Steve sat there until morning, and then I let myself into my house and fell into my bed that was sandy and salty and still damp with come.

THAT SUMMER I never went to bed unless I was high or drunk or both, and in the morning I pulled on my cut-offs and brushed my teeth and went out into the rising sun and down to the beach and swam. What it was, you crossed the road from my house and you were looking at open golden light with the beach going along and away east and west and never ending. It was blazing hot every day. Day after day the sea was flat calm in the morning. Every day that I sat in the sun and my skin darkened I got further away from the place I had come from.

I've found that the world tries to force you into closed places to live and work in and closed places to get you there and back, but if you've ever lived on the beach the world is always open at one end to light and sunlit water that goes away forever, and you look out and wonder and dream about just going out there, just to see what's at the end of it.

Scott told me once, they all tell you to think, the boss or your teachers, but just wait until what you think is different from them. Then you'll find out they didn't mean it. We were standing on wet sand just before dark as the tide went out and we couldn't hear the hum of the town for the rushing sound of the sea. What I'm looking for is out there, he said, nodding his head toward the darkening water. Me too, I said.

In the first days after the raid on the Ocean Wave I waited for something more to happen between the Persians and the skinheads but nothing did. Nothing I ever heard about anyway. Scott did not ask me about Dawn and her Dad again and I let myself think that he had forgotten or that he had not meant what he said. I got that wrong. I guess Scott just thought that he had asked me once already and he wasn't going to ask me again. That would be more like him for sure. Every time I did see him he gave me money and bits of drugs and that should have told me something, but I was in that space where everything was about me. I'd wake up to this bursting sunlit world. I was very tan and my hair grew longer and was sun lightened to strawberry at my shoulders. I was dumb with love for the beach, and the days ran into one another and were pretty much all the same.

Part of me had given up Dawn to the skinheads. I didn't think I could be what she wanted me to be even if I knew what that was, and I could only see trouble if I started asking her the questions Scott wanted asking. The thing is I'd told Scott I would, but you know how big talk in the night looks small in the day.

I lost myself to the beach and the summer sun. I loved it the most and I always have. If I think back to when I was a little kid I can't remember cold weather and that's the truth. I remember warm onshore breezes coming in the spring, bringing the salt smell of the sea to me through my open window in the early morning. And before school was finished for the year I'd be bunking off hot days to go to the beach.

You can't surf the beach where I'm from. It's the west coast that picks up the swells coming off the Atlantic. Where we are in the south the swells you get off the channel aren't strong enough to give surf, and the beach goes along east and west for miles in a gently bowed line so there are no point breaks. No land comes out to make them, and the low sandbar beach breaks we do get don't give the waves enough height to surf when the weak swells hit them. Scott says he's heard of people surfing Beachy Head; the chalk cliffs fallen into the sea in the last few years there make a small point. And he says in a strong onshore wind you might get surf at Brighton, but not where we're from.

So from when I was little I went to the beach under high blue morning skies to swim but mostly to sit under the sun and look out to the horizon. Smoke some Rocky and get a tan on. That summer I was so black I turned heads. I don't know why that was so important to me but it was. Taylor Beaumont, for one, wouldn't sit in the sun for longer than five minutes. But for me the sun is where my heart is the way God is for my wife, though like I say to her, I can see the sun.

I'd head for the beach in the morning while the sun was still rising. I'd swim and sit on the beach and let the hot sun beat on me until I fell asleep with my head on my rolled up T-shirt. I'd fall asleep dreaming and when I opened my eyes my hair would be wet and I'd be blinded by sweat and half in my dream of faraway hot lands. I'd wake to beach stones burning fire hot under my hands and on my toes where my old red beach towel wasn't long enough anymore. Waking up on the beach, to the sun and the light glittering on the water, kept a dream head on you all day. And I wonder now about whether I am dreamy and live right inside myself because I come from the beach, because it made me that way, or if it's only me who sits on the beach looking at the water and the light in a waking dream.

I liked to swim when the sea was high so that when you walked in the water was straightaway up to your waist. The water flat calm as far as you could see. The sun would be hot on my back and the water cold up to my waist. I would splash seawater in my face and taste salt in my mouth and push my wet hands through my hair and let the water fall from my hands. The blanket of sea went away to the horizon. I'd dive and hear the heavy roaring in my ears and I'd swim underwater and then surface to light air and swim out, the sun hot on my back and spangles of gold light in the water. Above the water there would be no sound except for my breathing and the sound I made moving through the water. When I turned my head to breathe I'd see my arm rising and falling, spraying water, and I'd see the flat sea and high sky as sunlit blocks of colour. I swam a long way. Mostly I swam out to the end of the Pier and then west to the Wish Tower and back again. I'd come into myself on these long swims. I'd sleep and dream in the afternoons.

Sometimes I saw Eddie Beer in the late afternoons.

When his Dad was drunk in the town and after him to beat him, Eddie wandered all over to keep away from him. Eddie took to finding me on the beaches I was hiding out on, way out to the east of town where nobody knew me. Eddie would always be in the Wagon at night, with Scott and Bombhead and all the other skinheads, because he knew his Dad wouldn't dare go there.

It's funny but it was easy to be with Eddie in a way it wasn't with anybody else. Being with anybody else made me tighten up inside. Eddie looked up to me. He was the only one who bought into my story. Because I was Scott's brother I would always be golden to Eddie.

One day we sat on the beach together. There was nobody around and Eddie took off his dirty T-shirt and sat in his Falmer jeans. The burnt skin on his neck and left shoulder glowed under the sun so that it looked like larva crawling over him. There were blood red raised welts and deep scars on his back. He had some blue dots and a crucifix tattooed in India ink on his right arm and *Eddie* on his left. His back and chest were pale and his arms were red. He took his boots off. His feet were black with dirt. The sun burned in me. Eddie picked at the dirt on his feet and he picked at the scabs on his head. He didn't smell good. His blue tattooed face marked him outcast from the world. From the world he lived in anyway.

"Why don't you swim?" I said.

"Nah." Eddie said.

I didn't want to tell him he could wash himself clean in the sea, that he didn't have to swim. I hoped it would come to him.

"Do you ever think about what's going to happen?" Eddie said.

"When?"

"Fuck I don't know. After the summer. When we're older."

"Sometimes," I said, "But I don't come up with anything. Scott says he's going away. Maybe I'll go with him."

"Scott's going away?" Eddie said.

Eddie looked frightened and I wished I hadn't said anything. It wasn't like I knew for certain what Scott was going to do.

"I don't know for sure Eddie. It's just something we talked about."

Eddie picked at his dirty feet for a bit and wiped the dirt on to a big beach stone.

"I thought we were going to run things. Scott said."

"Look, Eddie, I shouldn't have said anything. I don't know what's going to happen, honest. I'm out of it, really."

Eddie picked at his feet and looked around. There was a man walking the shoreline with two little kids.

"Hey Kim," he said, "Give me them sunglasses a minute."

I took off my sunglasses and gave them to Eddie. He held them in front of his face and looked at himself in the dark lenses. Then he put the sunglasses on and watched the family at the shoreline.

I said, "I'm going for a swim Eddie."

I walked down the beach and broke the perfect surface of the water. I swam until I was cold and then I came back.

Eddie was still wearing my sunglasses. I was a dark form in the lenses. I sat on the beach and watched the silver drops of water dry on my brown skin.

"Do you reckon you can get tattoos off you once they're on, Kimmy?"

I said I didn't know anything about tattoos except I was pretty sure they didn't come off.

"This is me forever then," he said. "My old man, I shouldn't let him beat me but I can't help it."

Eddie put his dirty shirt over his head so that it covered his face, and then he put my sunglasses on over the shirt.

"Look at me Kim" he said, his voice all muffled and strange, "I'm the Invisible Man."

We sat there not talking anymore until just before

115

dark. Eddie looked scared and I thought about all the things he was frightened of. His Dad, the sea, what was going to happen to him. He was scared of having a tattooed face. There were places he could have gone to where having a tattooed face would have made him somebody to honour. I know, I've been to them.

"Come on Eddie," I said, "Let's go to the Wagon."

In the heat of the long summer days I could pretend to forget how I was joined to Dawn and Scott and the skinheads, and to whatever was going to happen next. The night does come around though, and at the end of every day I was bursting to see them all again. I was not a good friend to Dawn but sometimes when she was drunk she would come home with me. There were more and more nights when she didn't want to see me and I didn't ask her where she went or who she saw. I told myself I didn't care as long as she threw a ride at me sometimes.

Somewhere round the end of July I was super tan and off my head and playing pool in the Painted Wagon. I'd had a big fight with Dawn that morning, I can't remember why, and I had spent the rest of the day on a beach by Langney Point with Eddie Beer, drinking pear wine and smoking dope under the burning sun.

My skin was still warm. I could feel in my face how dark I must be. I was wearing Scott's old *Pimps, Punks, and Hustlers* Clash T-shirt that was too small for me and tight on my arms that were big from swimming. I had on my same old Lee jeans and bashed up flip-flops. There was beach tar on my feet that had been there for days. My hair fell into my eyes when I was playing and Tony Angelino was calling me girl and trying to grab my arse when I went by to play a shot. I was repeat playing *Ace of Spades* that had somehow been left on the jukebox, and making impossible shots. I had to hold on to the table and keep sweeping the hair out of my eyes, but when I lined up a plant or a double I couldn't miss. I had started off playing with Eddie Beer but I was playing myself now. Eddie was sitting in the corner nodding out and picking the scabs on his head. His head looked like it was covered in red ants.

Scott was over with Bombhead, and my brother hadn't spoken to me, but sometimes I saw him looking at me hard. Other times I forgot he was there at all. Dawn was sitting with Gary Angelino and Gary was making her laugh. It burnt me up. I knew she was laughing so I would see her. I wanted Dawn and I didn't want her. When I looked at her, yellow headed, tiny, all dressed in black, flashing her eyes at Gary, I started spinning out. She sat in the light of the door that was open to the street and she seemed to float in front of me. The honey coloured late afternoon sunlight showed in the rising smoke of the cigarettes I was smoking one after the other.

Ace of Spades came on again. "Turn that shit off," Gary Angelino shouted. I held the cue out in front of me like a fighting stick and blew Gary a kiss. He jumped out of his seat and made to come at me and Scott sat him down hard. Scott was red in the face, and he got up and walked over to the jukebox and kicked it and kept on kicking it until the record stopped. Scott walked over to me and took the pool cue out of my hand. I tried to look over his shoulder at Gary and Dawn but Scott moved and blocked me so I couldn't see. I knew eveyone was looking at me and I tried to smile at my brother but I don't know how it came out.

Scott said,"What's wrong with you Horse?"

"Oh shit Scott don't start."

Scott said, "Is that all you got to say to me Kim, don't start Scott? I've been giving you all these dollars for weeks and you won't even talk to me. Now you're coming in here showing yourself up and me as well. Don't tell me not to start. You're three years older than Gary and twice his size and you know what? He'd still beat the shit out of you and because he's a skinhead and you're not I couldn't do anything about it."

Eddie Beer sat up in his seat and said, "Come on Scott don't fight with your brother. He doesn't mean nothing."

"Stay out of it Eddie."

"Come on Scott, please."

"Eddie," Scott said, "I swear, stay out of it."

Scott looked at me again. I might have been crying. He reached up and messed with my hair until it fell in my eyes. Scott stroked my head with his big hand. He pulled me close.

"You need to leave here Horse. I need you to leave for both of us, do you understand me?"

"I want Dawn Scott."

"She's not with him Kim. Wipe your face and go home and go to bed."

I turned and made to leave. Dawn flat out wouldn't look at me. Eddie grabbed his dirty jacket and said, "I'll come with you Kim."

"Stay where you are Eddie. Go home Horse."

Scott picked up something and held it out to me.

"Hey," Scott called, and I saw he was holding *The Outsiders*, "You forgot this."

He threw it to me and I tried to catch it and missed. I picked the book up from the floor and left the Wagon. I wondered if Dawn might follow me but she didn't and why should she?

Under the full summer moon I wandered up onto the seafront and east towards Langney Point. I walked along effing and blinding out loud. After walking for what I knew was a long way but which seemed to be no distance at all, I found myself in a wild pub on the beach called the Buccaneer, where the last of the Langney Rockers had made a stand. I don't know what I thought I was doing in there. There was a rack of Triumph Bonnevilles and Nortons parked up outside and shining under the moon.

The Buccaneer was done up like a pirate ship, with crossed cutlasses, black and red Skull and Crossbones flags, and paintings of crazy looking black bearded pirates with names like Henry Every and Stede Bonnet hanging from the walls. The men who drank there looked like they might have once raided the Spanish-American coast for sure. They were old men, in their thirties and forties I guessed, with scarred and caved in heads and gold hoop earrings and faces red with drink and the weather. They were dressed in red neckerchiefs and boots and dirty jeans and black leathers with the painted club colours flying on the back: a cigar smoking skull wearing a blood red bandana and grinning under a sewn on banner reading *Langney M.C.* They held their drinks with oil stained and tattooed hands. Some had fingers missing.

I was on the other side of drunk now and the Buccaneer was a kind of dreamworld, a place where I did and said things that if you put a pistol to my head now I wouldn't be able to remember. The motley faces of the Buccaneer's crew folded into one another in the smoky bar light. I do remember going outside to look at the sea. I wanted to show somebody the way the full moon made a wide and golden path on the black sea that went all the way to the horizon. I don't think I was scared. If I had come there with the skinheads there would have been a war there and then, but I was just a young drunk kid, no danger to anyone but myself or so I believed, and the rockers were happy to sit and tell me stories from the wars they had fought in when they were younger. Small local wars with the mods and first generation skinheads, wars quick and bright as shooting stars, that were forgotten by everybody but the boys who had fought in them, and who had made every short bloody episode into legend. I have been drunk like that many times since so I can guess I told some stories too in which, I bet, I made myself the hero.

There was no pirate ship belonging to the men of the Buccaneer at anchor on the changing moonlit tide, but if there had of been I believe I might have woken to find myself part of the company on board and joined to their purpose. I had an ache to go somewhere and do something, but I didn't know where I wanted to go and what it was I wanted to do.

The one man I do remember talking to called himself Alf. He was small, with a dark face grainy with what might have been motorcycle oil, a false blue eye, and long grey hair tied back and falling down his back to the belt of his dirty jeans. He wore a leather jerkin with club patches sewn on to it. He had no shirt on and his body was covered with tattoos. I don't know if his tattoos were faded then or if they are only faded when I try to think of them now. I do remember that he had a large pirate skull on his chest, with a cutlass in the mouth and a banner underneath saying *Dead Men Tell No Tales*.

Alf seemed to like me and it may have been him I wanted to show the golden path on the sea to. He had something to show me too he said, a trick, and he reached up with dirty fingers and took his false eye out of his head and dropped it in his glass.

"Now son," he said, "ask me if I want a drink."

"Do you want a drink Alf."

"Cor," he said, "Wouldn't I!"

He drank his pint off and picked out his eye. He wiped it on his jeans and put it back in place. He was laughing like crazy.

"Do you get it son?" he was howling, "Wooden Eye! Wooden Eye!"

Later I asked Alf if he knew Dug. I don't why I was asking after a man I never wanted to see again. I guess I had it in my head that I still might find something out about him for Scott and thought I was in the right place to ask. Alf said he didn't know him, even when I told him what I'd heard about Dug and the Angels in Newhaven. Later I saw Alf talking to a giant at the bar. The giant had a huge belly and a shaved head with a red nautical star tattooed on the crown, and a black hole in his mouth where his teeth had once been. When he saw me looking at him he elbowed Alf and the little long haired rocker turned to me and shouted, "Wooden Eye!", and howled again.

I looked away and opened my book and tried to read but the words danced in front of my eyes. The book had buckled and darkened with the sun and I could smell heat in the pages. I had read it so many times that hot summer it was sometimes as though I had Ponyboy Curtis and Johnny Cade at my side, but I knew I was alone. I was hiding from everybody and dreaming the summer away.

The last thing I remember is flying west on the back of the giant's bike. My hair blew out behind me like a red flag. We roared along the coast road towards the still bright lights of the Pier, and home, as the morning lightened to beaten gold in the east and a thousand evening stars slowly disappeared from the high and lovely southern sky.

ONE BRIGHT hot morning in early August when I had not
seen Scott or Dawn or any of the skinheads for going on
a week, I walked out of my house and down onto the
front. I thought I would walk as far east as Pevensey
Bay. I might even go and see the castle Al Babe liked to
talk about. I set off with that false free feeling you have
when you push everything out of your head but the sun
and the heavy swinging music of the sea. Everything for
me was always fucked and strange, which is not to say
much I know, just that my life was in my head and a lot
of the time I tuned out the world and what went on. You
know how it is when you're high all the time.

Bombhead was waiting for me up on the Pier. He
called out to me and I turned to the west and saw him.
You could see him a mile off and know it was him. His
hard head and big body were skylined dark against a
pale, rose blue morning sky, and he leaned against the
railing high above the sea and looked all spooky and
massive. I had hoped that everything would just go
away. The sky went on and on behind him. There was
no wind and the sea was flat calm and popped and
dazzled with sunlight. Far out on the horizon a small
boat moved without a sail. High up on the Pier
Bombhead loomed like a black storm cloud. When he
moved his head the sun flashed in his Foster Grants.
When he saw me he pushed himself off the railing he
leaned against and walked along the boardwalk to wait
for me outside the Pier. I couldn't turn around and go
back the other way now he'd seen me, so I walked
towards him with the sun warming my back and what
seemed like the sound of my heart thumping in my
head.

I know that Bombhead scared a lot of people but he
was always kind to me. He smiled straight off and
punched and grabbed me and we started wrestling and
knocking over flowers. He threw me down and sat
across me and started pulling my hair. A barefoot little

kid carrying a red bucket and spade stopped and stared at us.

"I've come for your hair little brother. This fucking hippy shit has to go. We can't have you walking around like this anymore Kimmy."

"Fuck off Bomba, let me up man."_We were sitting so that he was holding me against him. His arms were big from work and weights and he held me tight, and he was my brother holding me, like when I was little and I had said something that made Scott laugh and hug me. After a bit he let me up and we sat on a bench looking out to sea. He looked at his trousers.

"State of my Sta-Prest Kim, I'll have to go and change."

I knew that Bombhead had not come to see me to cut my hair or wrestle so I waited. After a bit he said, "Scott reckons the only way you'll talk to him is if I come and ask you to," and when he said it I felt like everything had turned to mud inside me. I had often felt like that before, like anything that might be solid in me couldn't be leant on or trusted.

"Scott kicked me out of the Wagon Bomb."

"Yeah, but not forever Kim. What's going on?" Bombhead said. "You've just fucking dumped Dawn, it seems like to her. Nobody sees you and when they do you're monged out. "

"Nothing's the matter Bomb, leave me alone."

"Well Kim I can't do that."

"Why," I said, "what's happening?"

I could feel the old excitement to know what Scott was up to now and at the same time I felt the pressure come on me again like Bombhead was holding a pillow over my face.

"The other night some Persian ran into the Wagon shouting about Nazis and ran off. Tony Angelino chased out into the street after him and got jumped by a bunch of them. Bit of an ambush. Tony was in a state. You know Scott can't stand for that."

Bombhead rubbed his dark face with his big hands.

"So now there's a big fight set up for Friday night on the bandstand. No weapons and no fighting until then. Whoever loses is supposed to stop dealing."

"What's that got to do with me?" I said it before I knew what I was saying. Bombhead shot me a look like he'd never seen me before.

"Kim I swear you listen but you don't hear. Like it or not you're in it Kim. Even if you walk away from your brother and Dawn you're still in it. You need to come to the Wagon tonight."

I didn't say anything and he said, "You need to talk to Dawn and you need to talk to Scott. That's what I'm hear to tell you. You listening?"

"Yes Bomb."

"You'll be there right?"

"Yes."

"All right then."

I liked sitting there with Bombhead. I didn't really want to hear what he had come to tell me but I liked sitting with him. I felt safe. Nothing was likely to kick off if you were with Bombhead. He was so tough he'd won a little space where he could be peaceful. Bombhead had nothing to prove was how I thought about it, and I wondered how that must feel and of course I wanted to feel like that too. He sat with his dark hands spread and flat against his white trousers. His boots were shined and planted on the ground. I bet he saw everything from behind his Foster Grants.

"I was talking to Al Babe," he said, "you know he was up at that school, the same as you, about four years ago?"

"Yeah?"

"Yeah, and he reckons that Anderson bloke is a kiddy fiddler. Well known for it."

I closed my eyes and remembered trying to swim in the dead black water of the basement pool while Anderson watched. The pool that had no windows and that stank. Being taken back to my room in the too late dark. It's not as though I have to tell you everything but if I could have a clear day at the beach, with nothing happening but the sun on me and swimming in the sea, then all that went away. But I've told you about that.

"You got anything you want to tell me Horse?"

"Does Scott know what Al said?"

"He was there mate, yes."

"What about Dawn."

"No Kim."

I didn't say anything else. Bombhead talking to Al Babe about me was too much. Bombhead looked at his high shined boots and breathed hard. Me and Bombhead sat looking at the sea, and after a bit he put his arm round my shoulder and we sat like that. In my head I was already running away. Bombhead saying that to me turned me to mud inside again and put my head back into bad places. Scott wanted me to come and sit down with him and talk things out, but I knew that I'd run. It was like when I was little and I used to wake up every night with my head bleeding. I knew it was going to happen whether I liked it or not. Starting from when I was about six I used to wake up every night with my face and bed wet with blood. The blood falling out of me every night and afterwards the taste of blood in my mouth. Not sleeping in case it started again. This went on for a long time and then it stopped when I was thirteen. They told me that my skin broke easily. It didn't start again until I was twenty or so but I always thought it would. I must have just picked at my face while I was asleep, don't you think?

"When you're locked up," Bombhead said, "there's all kinds of pressures on you to punk out you know? How you live in them places is all to do with whether you man up or not. Say you got something somebody else wants, a bit of smoke or some money say. They will try and take it off you and if you give your shit up without a fight, then it's just a matter of time before you're taking it up the arse, do you know what I mean? Them's the rules. And that's what your whole life comes down to. You got to fight or take it up the arse."

We must have sat there for a while. I could really feel the sun on me and there were more and more people coming to the beach so we must have. I know me and Bombhead smoked a bunch of cigarettes. I could taste them in my mouth for a long time afterwards. We didn't say much more but just sat smoking and looking at the sea. Bombhead didn't push it and when he asked me I didn't see any harm in promising him I'd come to the Wagon that night and see Scott and Dawn. When he got up to go I said, "Aren't you supposed to be at work?"

Bombhead looked at me all strange and said, "It's Saturday Kim."

I watched Bombhead walk away. People walked round him and then turned to look at him. Two tan girls in bikinis and cut-offs and flip-flops giggled and looked down when he passed. His boots were shined and he was high stepping. I jumped down onto the beach and dropped my towel and jeans on to the beach stones. I took off my T-shirt and dropped it and kicked off my flip-flops and went to swim.

Much later when the tide was out so that the sand beyond the beach stones was wet and dark and shining, I walked west along the beach with the Pier behind me and through the summer crowds towards the Wish Tower. I walked with the white hotels on my right and the beach and the sea on my left and the town behind me. The promenade was flat to the Wish Tower. People were leaving the beach and going home. There was that peace that comes on people who have spent the day at the beach. People were going home in slowly falling light with the feel of beach stones under their feet and with the light and sun and sea inside them. People were smiling and talking to one another gently and holding hands.

A couple of skinheads in boots and cut-offs came racing by on skateboards. I don't think they saw me and I was away from the skins beach. One of them was Gary Angelino and his face was tan and smoothed out and peaceful as he skated into the wind he made. He didn't think anybody was looking at him, and he let himself look happy because he was.

I came to the Wish Tower standing at the top of the rising lawns and facing the sea. The promenade went around so that the old fort was above me and I was in shadow, and then began to rise so that the beach was below me and then the Wish Tower was below me and I carried on climbing past a walk of fir trees.

I climbed until I was up above the town and the beach fell away and I was at the beginning of the South Downs Way. I don't know anything that's prettier than the sea with the sun on it, when you're high up and looking back. Something to do with how much of it you can see and how much of it is still to be discovered beyond the horizon. The wind came over the rise at me. The sky got closer as I climbed. In my heart I was walking away from everything.

I sat up on the downs. The humped landscape swelled around me like a green frozen sea I was adrift in. In front of me the world was open. I sat on the sun warmed, curving earth and looked out at the water going on forever. This was the top of my world.

I thought that I could hide out up there. It was far enough away from everything. The fort was too close to the town. If people were going to look for me they would look there and on the beaches but they wouldn't come up for me on the downs, not even Scott.

I needed to get into my house and grab some stuff but there were plenty of places I could sleep out up there. I started to think of the camp I would make for myself and then I remembered the girl who was found on the downs raped and stabbed over and over and set on fire.

I thought about Ponyboy and Johnny hiding out in the old church. Dallas Winston gives them some money when they first run away and Johnny goes out on the first morning to buy enough food and cigarettes to hide out for a few days. The boys cut their hair, and Johnny buys peroxide to bleach Ponyboy's. Cutting his hair makes Ponyboy sadder than anything. Johnny buys a copy of *Gone with the Wind* for Ponyboy to read out loud. I'd have liked to have a book to read and somebody to hide out with and talk to. I wished I'd remembered to bring *The Outsiders* with me. I knew the story pretty well though and I could tell it to myself. The trouble was that what was in my heart and what was in Ponyboy's were different, and I knew that was what really mattered, what was in your heart. I knew it was likely my story wasn't going to end up the way Ponyboy's does: in fiery glory.

As the night came I wondered what Scott would do. As soon as I thought it the mud feeling came again. I had kept Scott out of my head but now it was too late. He was in my head and running it through for me. He would be waiting for me in the Wagon. He'd ask me what I was going to do about Dawn. He'd push me about what happened with Anderson. He'd say there was a difference between being a runaway and running away. He'd want me to man up and do what he'd asked me to.

There was thunder far off it seemed. You ever been up in a place like that? Close to the stars and close to heaven? Well. You feel small is what it is. It gave me a kind of a sweet, sad fever to think about it. How can we understand the earth and our being here? I was young and alone and scared in the night and my head went back to Anderson.

With some boys I guess, the ones who scared easy, Anderson would have bullied them into it. With boys who had nobody he came on all matey. I knew one boy called Youngblood that he paid. With me he played at being my Dad. He worked away at it. He knew that was what I wanted. Back then there were all kinds of things I did to fill the hole inside. The worse thing was there was a part of me all the way back inside that wanted Anderson to want me. Now I get it that he had known all about me all along so I don't really hate myself anymore. I did then though. I was a little boat out in a storm and he came on like shelter.

He wore me down but I didn't give in, not really. At the time it seemed too tough to have to stand. One way or another we'd all been taken away from people we loved and he was rubbing his hands. Things are different now of course. Now I can say Anderson was nothing. Back then things got so crazy I ended up thinking the only kind of men there were were men like Anderson and Dug or my Dad and that idea was enough to put me in a bad place for a long time. It was like when you stand under a waterfall. You don't know there's anything else in the world but falling water.

This is not to say fuck you but that's all I'm going to say about Anderson. To say anything about it at all is just to tell you where my head was when I came home that summer. With Dawn I went back to her thinking I should have been more, something, I guess. Especially when she had changed and looked like a tough boy. What could I tell her? She'd think I was soft, a fucking girl. She did anyway pretty much but she'd really hate me if I told her about that. So would Scott and Bombhead. And I could never have told Mum, you're mad to think I could.

I suppose I thought if I could keep it in then Scott and the skinheads did offer me a way of taking something back, but only if I could win some of Scott's toughness for myself. I thought I'd blown that as well but maybe I could make a showing in the fight that was coming up. I know there's different kinds of toughness now but I didn't then. Being tough like Scott seemed like the answer and that's the way things were building up. It's the only story they tell boys. They don't tell us about love, just about being tough. So if you ask me if I'm sorry for what I did later, and Scott, like I say, never did, then I'd have to say no. Because I don't know that I'd ever have found out about love, which is what this story is all about. I don't want you to think that I'm holding your hand but it is, really. You'll see.

I was cold sleeping out of course. All I had were the

jeans I'd wrapped in my towel when I left the house and I put the jeans on over my cut-offs and put the towel around my shoulders. I sat this way and looked at the sky and watched for shooting stars.

The sky was lighter than the land. I lay in the shelter of a ditch made by a bunch of rabbit holes that had fallen in. There were almost luminous horned poppies, and yellow gorse all around, and the dark outlines of apple trees against the sky. I smoked some Rocky and sang my Mum's favourite song, the old Billy Fury tune *A Thousand Stars in the Sky*, and then the good feeling I had went away and I fought to get it back. I was hungry and thirsty. Sometimes there were pairs of small moving lights in the darkness and I guessed these were the eyes of foxes or rabbits.

You know how sometimes you'll say you're going to do something and you talk to yourself about it, and every time you think about what it is you're going to do your heart lifts, even though deep down you know that whatever it is you were going to do you won't?

I thought that if I walked over the downs in the morning I would be in another place. I could camp out at Cuckmere Haven. I could keep going all along the coast to Newhaven or even Brighton. I kept that thought inside me for a long time and from the high dark land I watched the moon on the water and then I tried to sleep.

I spent the night up there and all the next day and then I came down. I knew I would. It's like Ponyboy says, I lie to myself all the time, but I never believe me.

I CAME down and headed inland and walked along the wide avenues and big houses of Uptown. It was a different country. There were the walled gardens and I could smell honeysuckle. The streets were clean. You didn't see people. They were all behind the high walls I guess. The tall red brick walls made me curious. I wanted to climb and look over. I thought maybe I'd see happy families sitting on those white wooden chairs. They'd be talking to each other and drinking from those glasses with those holders they have to keep the drink cold. There would be a clean blanket on the lawn and a big friendly dog that was good with little kids. I couldn't hear anything though. Just these little birds singing strongly in the horse chestnut trees. A young smiley tabby cat stalked the little birds. The honey light was thick with floating seeds and downy tufts from summer flowers, and with flies fighting and fucking in constant swirling patterns. You couldn't see the sea but you could feel it in the high open light and you could taste it in the air.

I walked around and after a while I was in South Street. At the top of South Street was a police station with bars on some of the windows at the back. They knew Scott in there. I walked down the little hill from the police station to the library where when I was a kid Mum had sometimes left me in a big sunlit room with a pile of picture books while she went to work. She knew that when she came back I'd be where she left me. I was always crazy for books and stories the way I was crazy for the beach. I looked in through the big glass windows. I would sit on the floor by this window and read my books in the warm light the sun made. Books about cowboys and soldiers. I guess other boys would be reading these books now. The sun on the glass was too bright for me to really see in there. I could see rows of books but mostly what I could see was a reflection of myself looking in all dark and wild.

I stood in front of the window for a while pulling
stupid faces and looking at the books and then I sat
down on the lawn in front of the library. I smoked a little
single skinner and fell asleep in the sun. Later I walked
up to the Ocean Wave. I knew there would be Persians
in there and I had a story in my head. I thought I'd say
something or maybe even do something. I had
Bombhead saying there would be no fighting until
Friday so I wasn't really being brave.

A few heads turned when I walked in but nobody
jumped me the way I was half expecting them to. There
was a long bar on my right that ran the length of the
room. There were two pretty blonde girls serving drinks.
One of them was Cairo Angelino. She'd been a punk for
years but now she was a super tan beach girl wearing
short frayed cut-offs and a white halter-top patterned
with sky blue hibiscus flowers. Her sun-whitened hair
was coming in locksed up, and she had dressed it with
beads and shells and little brass rings. Cairo flashed me
a short smile and popped me a cold Breaker, "You sure
you're in the right place Kim? It is Kim, right? I mean,
you're looking pretty ragged man. I nearly didn't
recognise you."

I was wearing the T-shirt and flip-flops I'd left the
house in two days before. I'd wrapped my cut-offs in the
beach towel I carried and I was wearing my old jeans. I
guess I was dirty and crazy looking. There was chalk
and mud on my jeans and burrs in my long hair. My feet
were black like Eddie Beer's. I'd forgotten to swim
somehow, when I came off the downs.

"You're not here for trouble are you?" Cairo said.
"Your brother's not outside?"

"I'm on my own," I said. "I'm looking for somebody."

People were shouting hello to each other in rich
sounding voices across the crowded room. There were
some low tables set up on the bare wood floor and
people sat on big cushions. At the back of the bar there
was a wide iron staircase that spiralled up to the floor

above, and a procession of tan, long-legged girls in summer dresses walked up and down the iron stairs. People were stopping at tables to say hello. There were lots of people hugging and kissing one another. It was still light and the big glass doors were open to the terrace, and a soft and warm salt breeze folded in with the smell of honeysuckle feathering the room.

I walked past four tan blond boys laying out on cushions. Two of the boys wore Fruit of the Loom cords and the others wore faded Levi's. They were all wearing pastel coloured Lacoste shirts and Topsiders. There was a pair of Ray-Ban Wayfarers on the table in front of them and a boy with a lime Lacoste shirt on had a pair of Wayfarers pushed up on his head. They all wore bracelets of bits of coloured thread and beads and one of them, a boy with thick and waved sun lightened blond hair, wore a big silver watch. There were a couple of packs of soft-top Marlboro reds on the table. There was a bottle of wine on the table. Everybody was smiling. Everybody had everything I thought I wanted. Nobody had a tattooed face. I didn't recognise the up tune that was playing on the stereo that was kept behind the bar. Cairo Angelino was dancing with the other girl, Sandy something. They were dancing back to back and Cairo was holding her hair up and laughing. I walked through the room and went upstairs.

There was a heavy brocade curtain hanging down from the large French windows that opened out to the upstairs terrace. There were soft voices coming from the other side. I reached out and put my hand on the curtain, feeling the thick raised pattern. I lifted the heavy material and saw a group of Persians drinking spirits at a metal table. They wore gold watches and gold rings and necklaces and there were gold lighters on the table. The Persians wore open neck silk shirts and Benetton sweaters loosely tied around their shoulders. What they were drinking was gold in the glasses. A smooth, bored sounding voice behind me said, "I don't know that it's a good idea for you to go out there."

Hazim smiled at me like he owned the place and everything in it. His chocolate brown hair was blow dried and swept back in a tall pompadour and streaked with blond highlights. He had put something else on it that kept it stiff and still on his head. He was carefully unshaven and he had a dimple on his chin. He had thick lips and a nose like an upturned row boat and dark, sleepy looking heavy lashed eyes.

He was wearing a pastel linen jacket with the sleeves pushed up over a blue and white cotton shirt in something like a gingham check. He had on new, pressed, stonewashed Fruit of the Loom jeans and white espadrilles. He was smoking a Dunhill and he held a golden lighter in his right hand. In his other hand he held a cool looking drink in a tall glass. With all the gold he wore he flashed and glittered when he moved, and when I looked at him it was like when you're coming up on a trip and you get those little tracer flashes in the corner of your eye. His voice was like his hair. Rich and brown with white mixed in it.

"My friends might get the wrong idea, Kim" he said. "It is Kim isn't it? The little brother. We all know you. You stand out from your friends. I mean you could just be what you look like but in the circumstances going out there might seem a little provocative."

"What do I look like?"

"Like somebody who wants something for nothing. A poster boy for stoner wasters everywhere. What are you doing here? You want some smoke? Something better than the rubbish you're smoking now? I can get you temple balls, some Thai stick maybe, how about some co-caine? I bet you'd go for that."

He looked at me some more. I didn't say anything.

"No? So what are you doing here? You know there's no fighting before Friday. Your brother didn't send you. Maybe you just like it on this side of town. Is that it, is this where you'd rather be? Over here with us?"

I was going to say sorry I think, or something like it, for what I'd done my first night home. I'd had this idea, sitting on the little lawn outside the library in the sunshine, that I could stop the fighting. I don't know where the idea came from but it was like Taylor said, fighting was stupid. The more Hazim went on at me though with his expensive voice, the madder I got. I pushed my hair out of my eyes and stared at him. I couldn't think of anything smart to say. I said the only thing I could think of.

"My brother's going to fuck you up," I said.

Hazim laughed. He put his face in close to me. He was like money breathing on me.

"Will that make you feel better? I doubt it. Your brother can beat us on Friday, it doesn't matter, you know that. You give yourself away with your sad face. We'll still be rich and you'll be locked inside your skin and unhappy and faraway from where you want to be. Go on now, you aren't going to do anything. Go and be unhappy somewhere else."

He reached his hand out for the brocade curtain and lifted it and went outside, calling loudly and happily to his friends. I stood there on the other side of the curtain and listened to the strange sounds for a little while, and then I went downstairs to get another beer from Cairo Angelino.

Much later I was talking to a pretty blonde, tan girl in a summer dress. She was maybe nineteen, older than me anyway. She had big soft brown eyes and a gold locket around her neck.

"I was with this boy one time," she was saying, "and he came in my face. Then he went around saying he broke me in."

We were stood at the bar and she was buying me a Breaker and we were pressed against one another in the crush. In that light I could see the blonde hairs on her tan arms. I could see the bikini line where the colour of her skin changed at the top of her breasts. She said, "Aren't you Scott's brother?"

Ambre Solaire came off her in waves. I said that I was and I started telling stories about him like I always did.

How hard he was and the things he did. I wanted this
girl to think I was like Scott. I thought she'd take me
home if I could make her think that. Then I got sick of it
and stopped telling stories about Scott and just looked at
her. Then one of the tan blond boys in Wayfarers and
Topsiders called her over and she went over there.

I lost my towel somewhere. I was sitting on my own.
I was sitting and talking to one of the tan blond boys.
Then I was on my own again. I kept tripping over people
who were laying around on these big cushions. Dawn
came in. She was wearing her black Harrington over her
black Fred Perry, bleached out jeans and black boots. She
moved through all the smiling, blond, and tan people in
the bar and she was from somewhere they had never
been.

I couldn't think of anything to say to her that would
sound good or make her happy. She looked like she'd
been crying and had only just stopped. I never knew her
to cry before. She stood in front of me and I thought she
was going to hit me. She was smoking a cigarette and
the fingers of the hand she held it in were bitten and red.

"Where have you been?" she said.

I didn't say anything. I had nothing to say. I couldn't
believe she was in there.

"You're supposed to be with me," she said.

She kicked me and I fell on the floor. She kicked at
me as I sat on the floor. It hurt. I didn't try to stop her.
Nobody did. People watched. The boy with the
Wayfarers pushed up in his hair was laughing at me.
Dawn kept shouting at me and kicking me with her hard
little boots. She kicked me and threw her lighted
cigarette at me and shouted, "You're supposed to be my
friend!" I think I saw Hazim and some of the Persians
standing at the top of the iron stairs and looking down at
us and laughing. Dawn shouted, "When I need you, you
run away. All you want to do is fuck me!"

There was a big laugh when she said that. Cairo
Angelino came from behind the bar and put her arms
around Dawn. "All right mate," Cairo said, "You need to

leave right now." Dawn let Cairo take her outside.
People were clapping. Cairo came back in looking fierce
and pissed off. I started to say something and she said,
"I don't want to hear about it Kim. Save it for the freaks
in the Wagon like my brothers. I don't want to see you in
here again until you sort yourself out. I told you when
you came in."

I got up off the floor and went outside. People looked
at me like they didn't know what they were looking at
and would forget about me when I was gone. Going
outside I could hear people start up to talking again and
some laughing. I heard Cairo shout to the other girl
behind the bar, "Did you know that was a girl Sand? I
need a big drink with a fucking umbrella in it, Jesus. I
hate fighting man, it's such bullshit."

I CAUGHT up with Dawn and we went down to the beach. We walked on different sides of the street and we didn't talk but we knew where we were going. She stopped at the beach where I had first fucked her, west of the Pier and in front of the Mansion Hotel. Afterwards there were red marks on my knees and on the backs of her legs and her arse from the beach stones. I remember we lay beyond the lights of the hotel. I didn't care about her Dad then.

We sat on the front and the hotels were like snowy mountains behind us. Above us there were stars and aeroplane lights. Lights moved up and down on the horizon. There was a big summer moon like in a kid's drawing. There was no smell of vanilla in her hair and her hair was dark at the roots.

"Where were you anyway?" she said, "Me and Bombhead looked all over."

"What about Scott," I said.

"Oh Kim," she said, "You're such a cunt. Scott's in bits, what do you think? I even called your Mum."

I can tell you about Scott, I said, and I told her all about what he had asked me to do the night I came home. She listened and looked at me. There were hills of beach stones and dark valleys that made hiding places. I knew there would be kids fucking in the dark places like we had.

"I know what Scott wants," she said, "I don't know anything about that and I don't give a shit and I've said so. You think I want to know? I mean what is it that makes all boys think girls are stupid?"

She lit a cigarette.

"Scott's going to war now after what happened to Tony, and then I reckon he's going to go up against my Dad, and I don't want to be around for that. I reckon Scott wants to fuck him up and send out a message. I'll stay for the fight Friday but then I'm off."

"Where are you going?"

138

"You know my Nan lives in Croydon. My Mum's Mum. I'm going there."

She wanted to go back to school. She loved Scott and Bombhead. "I'll always be a skinhead now," she said. Being a skinhead gave her something to believe in. When she went to London there would be other skinheads and she would have a family straightaway.

I asked her why she was going now.

"Look Kim," she said, "I know you think you know what my Dad is like but you've got no idea. You think this is all some kind of a cool story. My Dad sits up there, he's off his head the whole time and he has kids up there, boys as well as girls, that he gives drugs to for fucks. One big party. That's what it's like up there all the time and I can't stand it anymore. I wanted to tell you Kim, but you weren't around and when you are you don't listen to anybody, so I told Bombhead."

"Not you then," I said.

"What?"

"He doesn't come after you, your Dad?"

"No Kim, he wouldn't. That just shows how little you know. He loves me. A big part of me just wants to fuck him up with Scott, but he's still my Dad you know? I mean he has always looked after me just in this crazy way."

He used to get her stoned when she was little. She was seven or eight. And she loved him. He was her Dad and it was just the two of them after her Mum went off with the biker she went off with and left them alone. So when she was little her and her Dad were together all the time. They used to go on runs together, just her and her Dad and a chopper and a tent to sleep in. They went to bike shows and metal festivals and sat around bonfires late into the night and she was ten and drinking Thunderbird and getting high, and she remembered the way the light from the fires burned in the eyes of the men sitting there and looking at her. He made her dance round the fire sometimes. She remembered metal bands and strippers and fire-eaters and men looking at her.

"You talk about not having a Dad but that's just something to hide behind. When things go wrong you always hide behind it as if not having a Dad or not being tough like Scott explains everything but it doesn't. If you were a skinhead, or anything, you wouldn't walk around the way you do."

She looked at me.

"I'm a skinhead," she said.

"Yes," I said.

"You were the only one I ever slept with."

"All right."

"I mean it," she said.

She was quiet for a bit.

"You know what I really hate?" she said.

"What?"

"That you believed me when I said I slept with all those boys."

"I'm sorry," I said.

Then we were both quiet.

"What do you want to do now?"

"I want to go on the rides," she said.

She meant Treasure Island. Treasure Island was an adventure playground east along the beach. We walked there. It was getting late. There was nobody around. There were lots of painted animals. There were lions and giraffes and hippos and elephants with the paint coming off. We jumped over the fence. There were painted black people in grass skirts and holding spears. She sat on the roundabout and I pushed her round. I pushed her until she was going round fast and then I sat on the grass and watched her go round. When she came round by me she talked to me. She came round by me and said, "I made myself look like a boy and you all want to fuck me."

She sat on top of a giant green crocodile. The crocodile had big pointy teeth and a red mouth and was in a little dirty stream. The banks of the stream were made of sand and the little stream was milky with all the sand in the water. Dawn pushed out the sleeves of her Harrington so that they came past her hands. She had taken her boots off and she sat on the crocodile with her jeans turned up high, flapping a cloth pretend hand up and down above the crocodile's back like she was whipping a horse. She walked barefoot in the shallow stream and she walked in the sand. She threw handfuls of wet sand at the crocodile. The sand balls she threw hit the side of the crocodile with an airy hollow whack and didn't stick but slid and fell down. She sat on top of the slide and went down head first. She kicked at the crocodile with her sandy, pale bare feet. She shouted at it. She sat on a swing and asked me to push her. I pushed her and she asked me to push her higher. She wanted to go all the way around. I pushed her and she kicked her feet, and she went up high enough so that the rope began to give on the upswing and then kind of drop her, but I couldn't get her high enough for the swing to go right round without dropping down. She jumped off and landed in the sand.

The summer wind blew gently in the rigging and masts of the sailboats pulled up on the beach. The soft metal ringing was like the sound of prayer bells I heard in a temple on the beach at Maui years later.

"Where are you going just now?" I said.

"I'm going to Bombhead's," she said.

We sat and turned our faces into the warm breeze coming off the sea. We could see the lights of a night fishing boat moving far out. I tried to hold her hand but she wouldn't let me. She was still angry.

She said, "You have to tell me what happened to you because you've been no use to me since you got back from there."

The boat went over the horizon and the lights disappeared.

"Kim, Kim."

I wondered what it was like, to be out of sight of land.

"What happened Kim?"

I had to bite down not to tell her. Everywhere I went people seemed to be fucking and fighting on each other.

She gave up trying to get me to talk about it. I flashed on the glory dream of taking Dug out and going back for Anderson. What was it with all the men? Men like Anderson and Dug and my Dad? And all the Dads that weren't there, who had run away, and the Dads that were there but who knocked you around or worse. How all that just built and built like a giant wave that tore up everything. I saw then for the first time how tough Dawn really was.

I said, "I do really like you, you know."

"I know Kim," she said, "It's all right. Go and see Scott, he's worried about you."

I asked her if she wanted walking to Bombhead's but she said she was fine. Walking away she looked more like a boy than ever and I thought about that. She was firing out messages it seemed to me, that would mean different things to different people. It must have really messed with her Dad's head to see her like that and maybe that was all she wanted to do at first. It would be the kind of thing you'd flash on if you were her. But then, I don't know, I was always surprised when anybody did something for a reason, had really thought about it I mean.

She looked like a boy for sure and you might think she must have looked kind of runty like Eddie Beer because she was so small, but she was a tough boy like Scott, you could tell by the way she walked, up on her boots and with her head up and with a hard look. And if it was a boy's look it was one that said she'd always been on her own and now I think that's the way she was most like a boy. And I knew she was alone and felt alone even when she was with me and that was what she had just told me. So I get it now, how much she must have loved being a skinhead, because that would be the best thing about it I guess, that feeling, however long it lasted, of not being on your own.

I WAS wiped out, like the way you feel for a couple of days after you take a hit of acid. I thought about getting away. Like always that was the first thing that came to me. What kept me there I guess was the sun and the water just as much as my ties to Dawn and Scott. The summer. I was just shot through with the heat that went into me and kind of bloomed and spread like blood in water and coloured everything. Where else was I going to go when everyday the sun blazed and the sea sparkled in high on the beach and back out over the sand? To a city? I knew it wasn't going to be hot always and I was finished with school and wasn't going back, but that just made me want to stay until the end of the summer. One day you would need a sweatshirt and that would be it, and unless you were a beachcomber like Steve Tardelli you'd stop waking up in a rush to get to the beach and then what? You'd have to find something else and I didn't know what that could be.

I looked at my skin, at my arms and feet black in the violet night. I was so dark people stopped to look at me. Maybe this was as dark as I was going to get. Maybe the colour had already started to fade. When it was gone I'd be the same as everybody else. I'd just be scared, that's all, not marked special by the colour of me.

Scott was getting out wasn't he? He was gone at the end of the summer he'd said. Why couldn't I go somewhere where the sun was still shining? All right I was sixteen but I'd be seventeen come the spring. I needed to find a bit of whatever Scott had that made him Scott, and then I could make myself into whoever I wanted. First there was the fight with the Persians and then Dug it sounded like. When Scott and Bombhead and the skinheads went after Dug I'd be locked into that too and I knew that Scott would take the chance to rip off whatever the biker had to steal up there, drugs and money, and that if I was in it I'd get a share. I would have earned it this time and whatever I got would help me get away. Jet off to somewhere hot, like Scott was saying. And then straightaway it kicked in and flashed in my head and I couldn't help it, that maybe whatever Scott had in mind would go wrong and we'd never get away, not me or Scott or Bombhead or anybody. We'd end up like men I'd seen in the Buccaneer. Men gone to fat and drinking the heart out of the day while the world went by outside. Talking about the glory days when they were tough and ran the town.

And what did Dawn mean when she said they were going to fuck him up? Fuck him up how? I had to go see Scott, and whatever it was I had to be in it because only then would I be able to leave with my head up. If I chickened out or messed up again in some way then even if I went somewhere nobody knew me, I'd always know that I wasn't a proper boy. Like with Anderson. It didn't matter that say Scott or Dawn didn't know about it, I knew, and I felt like I had been emptied out inside.

I lit a cigarette and walked back up the beach towards the Painted Wagon and Scott, walking back towards town the way Dawn had gone. I was sick of listening to myself. I had that falling feeling inside you get when you have to do something you don't want to do. I wanted to tell Scott that I felt like we were about to step up onto a plane I knew was going to crash. It was a long walk. What breeze there had been had died all at once. The night had become steamy, real sleep outside heat, and with no wind to break the surface of the water the waves came into the beach and out again in flat heavy blocks of school coat blue.

Scott was closing up in the Painted Wagon. When he saw me come by he made a face. I saw him. He was standing by the pool table. The honey light coming from the box over the table was the only light in the bar. Scott had a beat box up on the table and he was playing a *Tighten Up* cassette. Hash and lager were thick in the room. Scott was barefoot and wearing tight jeans with a high cuff turn and nothing else. He looked like a fighter

and that's what I believed he was and it was all I saw
that summer. He stood in the light counting paper
money out on the table. He counted money to an
amount and then he banded the short stack of notes with
a rubber band and started again. His tattoos and muscles
popped and moved under the light. Everything about
him seemed so certain and I wondered, like I always did,
how we could be so different. Now for sure I know that
he learnt certainty to protect himself and put himself
where he wanted to be. How else was he going to get
along when he had nobody to show him the way? It was
like being shipwrecked on some deserted island. You
could either sit in the sand on the beach and talk to
yourself all day, or you could make the hard climb to the
highest point of the island and try and take charge of
this new world.

"Where the fuck have you been," he said.

When I was with him he just took me over, as if his
hot blood got somehow mixed with mine across the
short distance between us. I don't why I was surprised, it
was the same blood.

There was an overflowing ashtray and a can of
Breaker on the table. The gold light was shining on the
worn cloth like late sunlight on burned grass at the end
of summer. Scott was smoking a joint and he held it out
to me. I stood way over by the door with my arms
folded. Scott shrugged and took another drag of the
joint. "Look," he said, and when he spoke great clouds
of blue smoke came from him and spread out in the
room, "It's going to be all right, honest."

His eyes were red. He looked like a young horse that
had run hard. Every room he was ever in was too small
for him. What was he then? Nineteen.

"Bombhead told me all about it," he said, "about her
Dad and all that. So everything's changed."

I didn't say anything. I wondered how you got to be
somebody who decided when everything changed. Did
you just say it had and get everyone to sign up for the
new plan? I was thinking that he was going to start by

cursing me out but he was all business, as if what he had heard from Bombhead was the excuse he needed to go after Dug.

"You heard we're fighting the Persians Friday?" He pronounced it Fri-*dee* like everybody else I knew.

"Bombhead told you right. Is that why you legged it?"

No, I thought, I ran away because I'm scared of you. I'm scared of being like you and I'm scared of not being like you. I don't know what to do Scott.

"No mate," I said.

Scott said, "It's the right time to make this move. Summer will be over in a few weeks. I don't know how long this skinhead thing's going to last and I want to grab what I can now before everything blows to shit. You know Coops from out in Hampden Park? He's just back from India and Nepal. He reckons you can live on five bucks a day out there. There's sixty miles of empty beach in Goa, Kim. Coops spent all his time playing football on the beach and smoking Temple Ball. Maybe I'll go there or there's places in Indonesia I've heard about. If I can put enough money together I'll never have to come back."

"I saw Hazim," I said, "up in the Ocean Wave. He was laughing about Friday."

If Scott was mad at me for being in the Ocean Wave he didn't show it. He didn't ask me what I was doing in there but he got hot in the face with what I told him Hazim had said.

Scott said, "He won't be laughing for much longer so fuck him. We'll just take Dug too now. You should have seen him when he came by here. I thought he was going to start in about you but Bombhead was raging. Me and Al Babe had to pretty much hold Bombhead back. He wouldn't let Dug have his money or say anything."

"What happened?"

"Dug come by to drop off the gear and pick up from us as usual. Bombhead told him to fuck his money and leave the gear. There wasn't much Dug could do but go with all of us here. I said to Bomba what was that all about and he told me."

"What do you think about it?"_

"Horse," Scott said, "she's a skinhead and a little tough nut, and he's a dirty greaser pervert. We're her family now and we got the right. What do you think, we're not going to stand up for her?"

For the story going on in his head this is what Scott had to say and he could say it without thinking, like a part he'd learnt. How much of it he believed I still don't know. By then I think everything was about getting out for him and doing it right so people would remember him.

"What happens now?"

"I think," Scott said, "that he's going to have to come back for his money, and that before he does we have to take it to him."

"You said everything was going to be all right."

"Yes," he said, and his voice went hard the way it always did when I was meant to listen to what he was going to say next, "but we have to make it all right. She's a skinhead, she's your girlfriend or she was." He looked at me like he didn't know me. "I don't get you Kim. Don't you want to fuck him up?"

Scott hit the joint again and drank some beer. He stuffed cash in the pockets of his jeans. "I mean, are you fucking in there Horse? What's up with you? It's like you've been asleep all summer. You need to fucking man up. Don't you think she's waiting for you to do something?"

I said I didn't know what I could do. I said that was why I'd come to see him. I said I was sorry I'd fucked things up. I was still standing over by the door. Scott looked at me for a little while and said, "You didn't fuck up. You're just not here. Everything with you is in your head. It always was Horse. Bombhead wants to burn him out and the only reason he hasn't done it already is I asked him to wait. I told him you had to be in on it. First though, we have to scrap the Persians. First the Persians and then the mad biker."

I couldn't take it all in. It made me buckle. I came into the room and stood under the light of the pool table with my brother. Scott was saying again that we had the right. We could smash up the Persians and burn Dug down and fuck him up for being a pervert because in the world we lived in, we had the right. I could see that Scott was glad to have a reason to go after Dug and I wished he would stop talking and just lay off saying we had the right. I thought about Dawn, and about Eddie Beer and how you could see the scared and lonely six-year-old kid he still was hiding behind his tattooed face, and I thought about the doped up boys and girls up at Dug's. I thought about Buckingham singing love songs, and Taylor Beaumont with his lifelong guard up, and then, remembering Anderson, his hands and mouth on me, I thought: if anybody has the right it's me.

Scott was pumped and high and starting to move in a stoned moonstomping style to the Aggrovators instrumental that was chugging out of the beat box. You could always tell Scott was fucked up when he started to dance. If I'd have said to Scott just then to remember when we were little and we had played on the beach, and if I had asked him to look at us there, talking about what we were talking about, he'd have looked at me as if I was crazy. When we were little he used to lay with his head in my lap and I would stroke his long hair.

Scott stopped dancing when the track ended and he was holding a stack of dirty notes out to me asking if I needed any money. He was standing under the pool table light that peaked like a sunlit mountain face. He was looking at me with his brick red dog head and I lost him just for a second, he was all dog standing there and my brother was gone. Then he was making noises telling me to go home. He was saying Mum would be worried and then he was calling out to me and I could kind of hear him but I was spinning out, and in the end I let him take me there.

I STAYED close to home in the days before the fight. Scott made it clear to me that I should keep nearby and I wasn't going to argue with him anymore. When my brother brought me home Mum raged at me for running away but Scott talked to her and she was so busy working that it wasn't too long before she let up on me. I didn't spend more than five minutes thinking about her. I just buried what we were doing to her.

The night of the fight me and Bombhead watched Scott get ready. We were in our room, mine and Scott's. Scott had sat in the bath for a long time and now he was standing in front of the full-length mirror he had brought in from Mum's room and he was wearing tight Levi's that had been hand washed and then sun-dried in the back garden. Below the big picture of Bruce Lee above his bed, Scott looked in the mirror. Bruce Lee's black hair was sweaty and he was shirtless and wearing black trousers. He had these three even spaced horizontal cuts on his ribs that looked like they were made by a big claw. The cuts were leaking blood but Bruce was in a fighting pose and his eyes were blazing. Under Bruce Lee Scott was slowly making forms. Scott was very tan and built from work and he knew he was too big for the room or the house or the town.

I watched him. He was so clean. He was fresh from the barber's and his crop was neat and razor finished. From being up on the roof all summer his hair was more blond than red. Beads of water from his bath flashed and glittered in his hair. He sat on his bed and put talc on his feet and put on white socks and put on his buffed up boots on. He laced the boots and turned up the cuff on his Levis just so and talked to me. He stood up in his jeans and boots. He stamped his feet like a young horse before a race. Bombhead sat on Scott's bed. Bombhead brushed at a mark on his Sta-Prest that only he could see. He looked at Scott and Scott looked at him and grinned. We were all coming up on some speed.

"Feeling good Scott?" Bombhead said.

"Yes mate, I'm up. You ready to go?"

"I could run through a wall for sure."

Near the end of *The Outsiders* the greasers have a big fight with the Socs. They call it a rumble. It's a rumble with no weapons like the fight with the Persians was supposed to be and the greasers call that kind of fight a skin fight. I'd read the fight part of the book the night before. I couldn't sleep and I read it through. Dallas Winston and Johnny Cade are still in the hospital after saving the kids from the burning church though Dallas busts out to be in the fight. Ponyboy is still pretty shook up and he keeps getting bad headaches but he wants to be in the rumble too no matter what. Darry is worried about him but lets him because it's only a skin fight. Ponyboy gets right into it and never seems to be scared which I thought was fake. The fight ends with the greasers winning and Ponyboy getting kicked in the head and then him and Dallas going to the hospital just in time to see Johnny Cade die. Then Dallas goes out and gets himself shot down by the police because he's mad about Johnny dying. What was funny was watching Scott and Bombhead get all dressed up because that's what the greasers did too. Ponyboy says that he and his brothers always got smart before a fight. They wanted to show that the greasers weren't trash but were just as good as the Socs were.

I was laying on my bed wearing my newest pair of Lee's and a clean white T-shirt and smoking a cigarette. Scott had told me not to smoke dope before the fight, and the speed he had given me was starting to flick in my stomach and behind my eyes and make my mouth thick. I guess Bombhead and Scott were feeling the same way and that made me feel close to them. I was pushing my hair into my eyes and fooling around and they were looking at me and Scott was talking to me.

"That's what it's like for boys like us," Scott said, "well you know that, right? You listening?"

"Is that why you're skinheads?" I said.

"It's about taking some pride in yourself Kim," Bomb said.

Scott said, "You can stay stoned and think you're nothing, or you can keep your boots shined and your jeans clean because you got some respect for yourself."

"People look at me and they see me, you know?" Bombhead was saying. "They remember me. They walk around me, not over me. Before, they wouldn't see me. I make them see."

You let things happen to you and they will. Take things in hand or be fucked forever. Man up or take it up the arse. I know that's what Bombhead and Scott believed. Scott was saying, "Every time I get up on that roof they've taken another day off me that I won't get back. I'm supposed to do that forever and stay poor while somebody else gets rich off me. Fuck that."

"Not for much longer brother," Bombhead said. They were both getting chewy off the speed. Scott took the cigarette from me and smoked. He looked at me.

"Where you going after this Scott?" I said.

"Not sure yet Horse like I say. There's beaches everywhere," he said, "you want to think about it Kim."

"Could I come with you?"

"We'll see," Scott said. He was looking at my feet. "You're not wearing them?"

I had my flip-flops on. "I was going to."

Scott looked at Bombhead and Bombhead smiled.

"Mate," Scott said, "put something else on."

"Why?"

"Why do you bloody think you dopey bastard?" he said. Scott looked around the room. "Put them on," he said, pointing at a beat up pair of basketball shoes.

"All right."

"You gonna be all right?" Scott said as I was putting the shoes on.

"Yeah."

"Just get hold of one your own age," Scott said. "You see any knives or bollocks like that get out of there."

151

"I'll be all right Scott, honest."

"OK Kim," Scott said, "don't get tough with me." He laughed and rubbed my head. I loved it when he did that.

"You ready Bomber?" he said.

"Always," Bombhead said, standing up and smoothing down his Sta-Prest.

"Right then," my brother said, jumping into a Bruce Lee stance, "let's go and fuck these Arabs up."

Then it was time to go. We didn't talk on the way to the beach. The speed helped block out the voice inside my head that was always telling me I was shit. I was moving to catch up with myself, everything thumping in a fast and rising beat inside. Scott put his arm around me and we walked like that for a while. I had to fight. If I couldn't fight with what the stories pushed at me about being a boy and being Scott's brother and all of that, then what kind of boy was I?

The skinheads were waiting for us up on the bandstand. The bandstand was on the seafront between the Pier and the Wish Tower and we walked through a sun bleached, wood framed glass door into the amphitheatre that looked towards and up to the stage. The blue and white deckchairs where people sat to listen to band music were stacked against the back wall leaving an empty space to fight. There was a plaque on the wall in memory of a bandsman named John Wesley Woodward, who was playing on the Titanic when it went down.

The sun was setting above the downs in the west. There was a soft onshore breeze that made the waves have white horses. Under the turquoise domed roof the Angelino brothers, Al Babe, and Eddie Beer waited on the stage. The last of the sun flashed in the stainless steel spire on top of the roof.

Eddie Beer was dressed in the same clothes I always saw him dressed in that summer: his dirty T-shirt and Falmers and steel toe caps. Maybe he didn't have any others. In the rosy sunset light the burnt skin on his neck

looked white and shiny and hard. He wasn't wearing his
Harrington. None of the skinheads wore jackets. Scott
said you needed to be able to throw a punch and jackets
got in the way. Eddie was standing next to the Angelino
brothers. Gary's monkey face was set to a deadpan,
hardnut look. He yawned and spat into the white and
violet petunias that garlanded the stage. I couldn't have
raised a spit if you'd paid me. There were some bruises
on Tony's face that were beginning to yellow. Al Babe
was wearing a white Fred Perry and white Sta-Prest and
shining Docs. Al was golden haired and super dark
against his white clothes and I knew that was why he
was wearing them. Dawn was leaning against one of the
four blond columns that made up a colonnade
supporting the half-circle shaped roof and when we
walked into the amphitheatre she whooped and jumped
down from the stage onto Bombhead's back. Bombhead
spun her round and she laughed and he put her down.

She was dressed all in black. I went over to her and
said hey.

"Hey," she said, "You ready for this?"

I tried to laugh. I said, "What do you reckon?"

"Try not to think about it. Stay close to Scott. You'll
be all right."

"What about you?"

"Bombhead wants me to help if they team up on
him."

"You still going to London?"

"Tomorrow. I called my Nan."

"OK then," I said.

We hugged and I tried to hold her close. She held her
body tight so it wasn't a proper hug. After a bit she
broke away and that was supposed to be it between us.

With the red sky and the darkening sea at their backs
the Persians came from the walkway that went around
behind the bandstand and that was open to the sea but
separated from the bandstand by glass windows. We
watched them walk along and come into the
amphitheatre of the bandstand from the opposite end of

the front to us. Hazim was in the lead and, as he had
been the night I had seen him in the Ocean Wave, he was
smiling. I stared at the heavy gold rings on his fingers.
Most of the Persians were wearing big rings and they
had taken off their gold bracelets and necklaces and
watches. They were dressed in pastel Lacoste shirts and
chinos and Topsiders. I counted Ahmed, and there was
one big Persian who looked like a fighter and was
standing just behind Hazim. The big Persian's face was
thick featured and hard looking like a wooden mask. I
counted eight of them all together. There were seven of
us.

We stood still facing the Persians as the summer
evening crowds moved around us like water against
rocks in a falling tide. There was a group of young girls
wrapped in beach towels who were openly watching us.
I picked out a tall sallow boy wearing jeans that were too
short who was standing at the back of the bandstand
near the plaque for John Woodward. The boy's black
hair fell into his eyes and he had no rings on his hands
and he was watching everything. He felt me looking at
him and he looked back from under his hair and
breathed out heavily as though he were adjusting a
heavy weight he had been made to carry.

Scott and Hazim stood together.

"All right Hazim," Scott said. I could see his jaw
champing with the speed and I knew he was biting off
all the things he wanted to say.

"Hello Scott."

"No weapons like we said."

"As you can see."

"Tell them to take their rings off," Eddie shouted in a
high nervous voice.

"Shut the fuck up," Scott said, and then to Hazim he
said, "I can see all right."

I saw Bombhead slip a knuckle duster over his right
hand. It was made of dull curved metal with four round
finger holes and a taped grip. I had never seen one
before but straightaway I knew what it was. Hazim was

taller than Scott and older too, but Scott was wider and built bigger and more used to fighting. What have the Persians ever had to fight for?

A black headed gull swept around the roof of the bandstand and I could see the blue of the roof reflected in the wings of the bird. The gull cried and the big Persian with the thick head who was standing next to Hazim made a move as though he had heard a voice. Bombhead did not hesitate but sprang forward and hit the Persian with his metal fist. The big man went down like he'd been unplugged and he lay still with blood starting to spread across his face. Somebody screamed for real this time. Bombhead put the boot in. His boot went into the bloody face like the bumping head of a black shark feeding on meat. Fighting started up all over but a couple of the Persians looked like the heart had been taken out of them there and then.

Dawn shouted as Ahmed made a run at Bombhead from behind him. Bombhead turned and kicked Ahmed in the balls and lifted him off his feet. Ahmed fell and somehow got up on his knees. He kneeled with his mouth open in a silent scream and Eddie Beer ran at him fast and kicked him in the head with his steelie and Ahmed fell back and blood flew up into the air in a misty spray. Eddie ran around Ahmed in a war dance style.

The Angelino brothers were outnumbered by three Persians and Tony was getting another beating. Dawn jumped on the back of a Persian who was driving Tony back with punches and Bombhead waded in and cuffed a couple of smaller Persians Gary was just about holding off. Bombhead cuffed them with his left hand. Al Babe was in a one on one and getting the better of the boy he was fighting.

Hazim went after Scott with high spinning roundhouse kicks that Scott mostly blocked with his big hands and forearms. Scott moved inside Hazim's kicks and landed with short right hand punches to the Persian's face. Scott had heavy hands and he opened up

Hazim straightaway and blood flooded down and a spurt of blood hit Scott in the face like Hazim had spit at him. I heard blood splash on the floor. Scott rocked back on his heels and moved out of range. Hazim came for him with more kicks. He connected and snapped Scott's head back but did not cut him. Scott caught the next roundhouse kick and held Hazim's foot and leg and spun him round so that he was facing the floor and my brother lifted and pushed him down like he was emptying a heavy barrow full of hot tar onto the floor. Hazim hit the ground pompadour first and slid, and the skin on his forehead and nose peeled back and off. I heard the air go out of him as he hit the ground. Scott straightaway began stamping on Hazim's head. Bombhead, with blood dripping from his metal fist, shouted "They're running!"

Everywhere the Persians weren't on the ground, they were running. The voice in my head was screaming at me to move before it was too late. I went after the tall sallow boy who had been watching all this time and who was running now. I jumped on his back and we fell into a pile of deckchairs. He lay on his back and did not try to fight and I punched him in the face. I punched him again as hard as I could. When you hit someone in the face your fist gets bigger and the face gets smaller until there is just the fist. I hit him again and I felt something in his face break like thin china under my hand and he yelled through the blood in his mouth and I yelled along with him and I shouted at the reddening sky.

Scott was shouting my name. Gary and Dawn were holding Tony Angelino up and they were all looking at me. Tony had blood down his shirt. Scott was still shouting. The kid I'd hit crabwalked backwards and then turned and ran, crying and holding his broken face. A great wave of happiness went through me with a rush from the speed. There was a family of sunburnt out-of-towners looking sick at Hazim laying spoiled on the ground. A fat girl carrying a doll in a papoose on her back was trying to help him up. She was standing in the blood that was pooling out from his head and there was blood on her plastic jelly beach shoes.

The squad of skinheads had fallen back and moved out. The plan was to meet up at the Wagon and the thing to do was to find your own way there by the little roads that ran inland from the beaches and the white hotels. Julie Spanish and Galley Mouratidis were waiting for us. I kept off the front and away from bright lights. I was happy. I reckon I had proved myself. I had laid hands on this kid and made him bleed and I thought that should be enough for Scott.

There were no lights showing in the Wagon and I had to knock on the door for what seemed like a long time before Al Babe let me in.

"Here he is Scott," Al Babe said, "Crazy Horse."

Galley had put out some tea lights. Skinheads were sitting around smoking Rocky and drinking Breakers. I didn't see Dawn. Scott was over at the bar free pouring rum into a pint glass half full of ice.

"Did you see me Scott," I said.

"I saw you beating on some kid," Scott said.

Julie was holding ice wrapped in a bar towel up to Tony Angelino's face. Tony looked at me with one eye.

"Fucking dick," he said.

Scott said, "What did you think you were doing?"

I couldn't understand what he was talking about. I was flooded out with speed and buzzing and I didn't understand why Scott wasn't smiling at me. He wasn't looking at me and he was brick red.

Bombhead said quietly, "That kid you smashed up wasn't a Persian Kim."

"Don't fuck about Bomb," I said, "of course he was," but as soon as he said it I knew it was true.

"I'm not Kim. He was just some kid."

"He looked about fourteen," Tony said, "if that. See the size of you and you take on some kid two years younger than you and half your size. You're some tough nut."

The skinheads were laughing at me and looking

pissed off too. Nobody cared if the Persians and the skinheads fought each other but if somebody who wasn't involved got hurt, especially if they were from out of town, the law would come down heavy on the skinheads. Plus he was just a kid. I felt his face break again under my hands. My stomach flipped and I thought I was going to be sick. Scott drank deeply from his big glass of rum and paced up and down like he was in a cell.

"Scott?" I said, "Scott I didn't mean to, I thought he was one of them. I didn't think."

"That's all I hear from you!" Scott shouted, "I didn't mean to, I wasn't thinking! It's time you fucking started thinking. I can't carry you forever Kim."

"Scott," Bombhead said, "not in front of everybody."

"Stay out of it Bomb, you're too soft on him. He needs to hear it. You fucked everything up Kim and I've had to carry you all my life. This is it. I don't want you hanging around no more. Go home to Mum and get the fuck out of my sight."

"You're not my Dad Scott you can't tell me what to do!" I shouted at him, "I just wanted to be like you!"

Scott kind of whirled on me then and knocked me clear across the room and down onto the floor. I sat and looked up at him through tearing up eyes. Scott had never hit me before. He stood over me with his big fists slowly opening, Dawn and Bombhead and the skinheads kind of frozen and looking at him. I knew why Scott wouldn't tell me where he was going at the end of the summer. He wanted to be free and he couldn't be if I went with him.

I RAN into the night. I heard Bombhead or somebody shouting 'Horse!' as I ran along Seaside Road but I didn't stop. Down the side streets I saw the sea in these little flashes, moonlit and sparkling and high in the night and always there. I couldn't hear the sea over the roaring in my head. I stopped running. My head was stinging and my face was wet with blood. Seaside Road was long and wide and I could see all along it and I was alone. The sky was violet and star-filled and the streetlights had those starbursts of light around them they have when you look straight at them and your eyes tear up. In the starlight the pavement sparkled silver. I knew it was late but I didn't know how late.

Dug's garage was on a little dark side street. The place looked different in the night. In the day when I had gone there with my mother I hadn't noticed the wide, tall, chain-link fencing that surrounded the yard. Two sections of fencing that must have been folded back in the day to make an entrance were now closed with heavy padlocked chains. The yard looked empty in the moonlight but there were lots of dark places where the light did not fall. There seemed no way in but over. The fence was high. There were two lock-ups where Dug kept his bikes and tools and the bikes and cars he worked on. Above the lock-ups were the rooms where he lived with Dawn. There was a light showing in the room at the front. I had never been up there before. Dawn always came to me. I didn't think there was a dog. She would have said. I had to think what to do. I tried to think like Scott and the blood rushed inside me, filling my head. I reached out and lightly touched the fence and the fence made a sound like glass breaking in another room, all the way up the fence and along and into my head. No dogs barked. No more lights came on.

The other way I was going to get in was over the wall at the back of the lock-ups. The wall was one side of an

alley. I went around there and walked into the alley.
There was dog shit and piss and jasmine. On the ground
below the dark back window there were empty beer
bottles and beer cans. Some of the bottles were broken
and I thought that Dug must have thrown them out of
the window. There was a pair of pants on the ground
with a dark mark in them that I thought must be shit or
blood. It was too dark to tell. There were used Johnnies.
There were pieces of brown glass lined up on top of the
wall, broken and jagged like mountains in the distance.

I squatted down with my back against the wall. There
were some rags shining with oil. The blood rushed in
me. I collected the rags and the bottles that weren't
broken. I stuffed rags into the necks of the bottles. I lit
the first rag with my lighter and the flame lit up all the
shit in the alley, and as I stood there with the flaming
bottle in my hand Dug stepped into the light I had
made. He was carrying something down by his leg and
he lifted it and swung it at me and my head exploded.

When I woke I was in the black dark and my feet and
hands were tied with cable ties that cut into my wrists
and I had pissed myself and pissed the cot bed. The
sound of a motorbike going away had made me wake
up. Where he had hit me my head was soft and big and
there was a hard pain underneath. I touched my face
with my tied together hands and I could feel the dried
blood there and then sticky blood where the cut was. It
hurt to touch the cut but I couldn't help it. The cut felt
too big and I didn't know if that was because I was
scared and couldn't see it or because it was really big.
Then I felt my head because it felt different and my hair
was cropped right down and I cried. I was so thirsty. I
slept again and woke and slept. I knew it was her bed. It
was too small and I could smell vanilla and I could smell
her.

I was drowning when I was sleeping. When I slept I
saw Dug again in the lit up alley. I saw the fire I held
shining in his black eyes as two little points of moving
light. His long black hair was braided and he wore dirty

jeans and motorcycle boots, no shirt. In the flaring yellow molotov light his Angel tattoos danced like war paint. In my sleep the winged Death's Heads and spider webs left Dug's body and came flying for me across the alley.

Across his chest I saw tattooed the flag of the pirate Stede Bonnet that I had seen hanging in the Buccaneer; the Death's Head with the heart and cutlass either side and single bone below. When I woke it was all in a moaning rush for air. Like when you're breath hold diving and are coming up to faraway air fast as you can. The water lightens in spangles above you and you can see the surface of the water and the sunlight all spread out above, and you break the water and breathe hard and grateful. But every time I rushed up out of sleep there was no light. I felt burnt inside. When I was awake my head hurt worse and worse until, in the end, I couldn't fall back to sleep and I lay there until he came. The noise in my head had gone. My head was full of him now.

These are some of the things he said when he came.

He said he was sorry he'd had to cut my hair but I looked young and pretty without it and he didn't like long hair on boys.

He said that he'd told Scott to come on his own and that if Scott didn't come he'd take me down to the beach and shoot me.

He said Scott was queer for Bombhead.

He said he sent Scott my hair so Scott would come.

He said he wanted his money.

He said as soon as he had the money he was off.

He stuck his thick dirty cock in my mouth and fucked me in the mouth for a long time. My head banged against the bed while he was doing it and started bleeding again. When he came he pushed himself further into me so that I coughed it up.

Waste of spunk, he said.

I waited after he had gone and then I rolled off the cot bed with my hands still tied and crawled over to

where a faint line of light glowed under the door and I
got to the door and lay down so that my face was side
on to the floor and I looked closely at the light. More
than anything I wanted a drink of water.

I thought that if I looked at the light he wouldn't
come again because before he had come in the dark.
Then there was no light under the door and there was no
light in the room and no light anywhere. I think that I
must have shouted then but nobody came.

It was hot in the room and I could smell myself and I
could smell him. The smell of vanilla had gone. I began
to crawl over the floor in the dark. I wanted to find
something to stop him with when he came again. I
started by kneeling in the corner of the room so that a
wall was on my right and I could bring my tied hands to
touch the door handle on my left. I crawled naked over
the dirty floor and far away I heard Dug and Brian
Wilson starting to sing *Wouldn't It Be Nice*. I crawled
over the floor along dark imagined beaches and Dug
and Brian Wilson sang *You Still Believe in Me* and *I Just
Wasn't Made For These Times* and *Caroline No* and I heard
all the words and they made a story and then after
Caroline No ended the story was over and the music
stopped and I was alone again in the dark with nothing
to stop him. I pushed the bed up against the door as best
I could and waited for him to come. I couldn't keep him
out.

This time he pissed on me before fucking me in the
mouth. Keep it all in this time, he said, or you'll be sorry.
He said he was going to pump me up with some gear
and get some men he knew round who'd like me. He
tied me back up and tied me to the bed.

I lost some time after that. I guess I closed down. And
for a long time afterwards I tried to remember what
happened but there's nothing there and you might think
that's a good thing. I've had some blackouts since, for
different reasons, and I've learned that there's no getting
the time back. You step into another world for however
long and come back and whatever happens there stays

lost. The story of your life is broken and starts again. Who's to say you're the same person when you come back? I was being fucked in the mouth and then there's nothing. I don't know if he did what he said he would. I don't think anybody else came but I'll never know. I can't think about that. What I mean is that I thought about nothing else for years but I won't think about it now. I hope you can understand that.

What I remember next is everything all at once but just pictures. Fire and shouting and the door opening to light and Bombhead dragging Dug's body across the bloody floor as burned black paper twisted down on to Bombhead's bent back. The paper came slowly down and Eddie Beer sat against the wall drawing horses in blood on his jeans and I could not tell if Dug was dead or alive. The blood on the floor and the blood on Eddie and the blood on all of them came from Dug. He looked dead when Bombhead dragged him and I hoped he was. He was naked and swollen and red with blood and his body made a slurping noise as it was dragged on the floor. That slurping noise is the first noise I remember after coming back. Then Dawn was looking at my hair and talking to me. I was the only one bleeding, from the cuts on my head that Scott and Dug had given me.

Then I was holding onto Scott tightly and he touched me gently like he was brushing the hair from my eyes and carried me out into the late summer night. I thought I could hear the sea but then I don't know, it might have just been something I heard inside me.

"Did you kill him?" I said. My voice had gone deep and rough like Scott's.

Scott just carried me and shushed me. I was a foot taller than him.

There was a pale Cresta outside. Gary Angelino behind the wheel.

"Get the door open Gaz," Scott said and Gary reached back and opened the door. Scott put me in the back seat and got in the front next to Gary. It was a hot night and it was hot sitting in the unmoving car.

"Don't ever tell anyone what happened," I said. "Please Scott."

We watched Dawn and Bombhead torch the flat and the bikes and Scott laughed. Scott let out a long breath and rubbed his face. Dawn and Bombhead got into the car.

"Let's go," Scott said. Gary pulled out of the garage and drove down to the beach. The streets were empty. We got to the front and Scott said, "Park up here Gaz." Gary parked and stopped the engine and Scott said, "I need you all to get out of the car. Gaz, wait here and when me and Kim leave the car get shot of it."

"All right Scott," Gary said, and he got out of the car and stood with his back to us looking out to sea.

"You need to say goodbye to Dawn," Scott said.

I couldn't look at her. She put her hand against my face. She was crying.

"Bye Kim," Dawn said. She got out of the car with Bombhead and I never saw her again.

Scott got in the back of the car and looked at me. He put his hand on my head and rubbed my short hair. We sat that way for a while and then he pulled me towards him and let me hug him and I kind of pushed my face into his chest. We sat that way for a long time and then he helped me out of the car and we walked slowly down to the beach.

There was a fire on the beach and there were a few skinheads sitting around drinking Breaker and smoking pot. When they saw Scott and me they made room by the fire for us. I looked around. They were all younger than me and I didn't recognise any of them.

There was no wind. The tide was out. The moon was fat and pale and high like Dug's face way above me in the dark night. "You want a cigarette Kimmy?"

We smoked and I did that shaking thing you see people do.

I was barefoot and wearing Levi's and Scott's Harrington.

Scott said, "Sit nearer the fire." Close by there was the

wumpfh and pop of a small explosion. After a bit Gary
Angelino came and sat by the fire. Scott nodded to him.

"Did you kill him Scott?"

"No Horse, we didn't kill him."

"I wish you'd killed him."

"No mate," he said, and I looked at him. He looked
like he was coming off a rush. His eyes were red and
there were cuts on his hands. He looked like a boy.

After a bit I said, "Can we just go home Scott?"

Scott got up and brushed himself down and all this
golden sand fell off him and I got up and we walked up
the beach. The car was burning where Gary had parked
it. We walked home. We went in the back door. The
house was dark and quiet. We went up to our room. I sat
on my bed. Scott said, "You want some music on?"

The window was open and I could hear the sea. I
shook my head. Scott left the room and came back with
some iodine and cotton wool and cleaned my head up.
He brought me some water and I drank a lot of it. He
made me get into bed and he skinned up and gave me
the joint and an ashtray and said, "Smoke this."

Scott sat on his bed and watched me smoke. After I'd
finished the joint Scott just sat on the bed and watched
me. The onshore wind made the pale curtain dance in
the dark room. I tried hard to listen for the sea and for
the trains going away. Bruce Lee glowed on the wall and
I looked at his picture for a long time. I think Scott was
waiting for me to talk. Later when Scott was asleep I got
up and was sick for a long time. In the morning there
was blood in my bed. Scott clipped my hair down to a
number one but he wouldn't talk to me.

SCOTT HAD gone crazy when Dug had come by the Painted Wagon. Dug kicked in the blacked out window and threw in a bloody bag with my hair in it and roared off on his bike. That's what Bombhead told me when he came to meet me up by the Pier. I say Bombhead but he told me not to call him that anymore. Bombhead's a story that's finished he said. It was just before dark and the Pier lights were on and at my back the early winter breeze was edged with cold. Out to sea the lights of a working boat pitched slowly up and down. I was wearing Scott's black Harrington done up over one of Scott's Ben Shermans, Levi's, and a pair of Scott's black DM's. I'd been wearing the same clothes for weeks.

My hair was coming in kind of suedehead looking and I didn't know whether to have Eddie cut it again or let it grow out. I wasn't doing anything. I was just smoking cigarettes fast one after the other and watching the sea that was coming in grey and slappy and so high on the beach that I could feel the salt spray on my face. The sky was broken orange over the downs to the west. I saw planes going away up there. Scott was on remand in Lewes prison. I hadn't heard from Dawn and didn't expect to. Neal had letters from her. She was in Croydon. She told him that the skinhead scene was big there. I was going away forever too, just as soon as I got myself together.

Neal was wearing a white Sergio Tacchini tracksuit top, pale Lois jeans with unstitched and picked out frayed hems, and fresh white Diadora trainers. He hadn't cut his hair in a while and it was styled in a side parting and he'd put something on it to keep it smoothed down. He kept kind of patting it down with his big hand while he was talking. I asked Neal all about it.

Neal said Scott had called him and said Dug had got hold of me and to get round right away. Neal called up Al Babe to meet up at the Wagon. He called up the

Angelino brothers and told Gary to get a car. The Angelinos picked him and Dawn up in the stolen Cresta and they went round there and Scott was punching holes in the walls. When Al Babe turned up Eddie Beer was with him and Scott didn't want him there, looked at him like Eddie was a kid who'd come in with shit on his shoes, and Eddie said, you got to let me come Scott. I'm a skinhead and Kim's my friend. Come on then Eddie boy, Scott said. let's see what you can do.

They sent Eddie to skate over for a lookout. Then they drank Breakers and Gary had some sulphate that they split and they talked and then they got in the car and went over there. Everybody was talking at once, all crushed up in the back and flashing on the streetlights that flooded the car as they passed them by. Scott was coming up brick red Neal said, the way he does, and sitting next to Gary in the front. Scott kept turning to look at us, and you could hear his teeth working with the speed. They parked up the street from the garage and walked round to where Eddie was waiting. Eddie told them there had been a light in the window. He said there'd been some music but now it was quiet. Dawn was skipping from foot to foot. Come out of the light girl, Neal said, he'll see you. I hope he sees me, Dawn said, I hope he sees me with you, but she came out of the light anyway. She had loved her Dad and now that love was gone and she was ready to explode.

Scott had the Angelino brothers cut the fence and hold it still while he and Neal went through and across the yard and let themselves into the house with a key Dawn had given Neal. Crossing the dark yard with Scott Neal said he looked back towards the street. All the skinheads by the fence were smoking, even though Neal had told them not to. With the small burning orange lights Neal said it was like he was night swimming far out, and looking back at the lights of the town. It was like I was nearly out of sight of land.

How did Scott look crossing the yard? He had his face stuck out, Neal said, like his nose was opened up to

something he was hunting down and meant to find.
Dawn told them how the house was set up. The boys
crept up the stairs and waited outside Dug's room while
Al Babe made some noise out front in the street,
shouting out and carrying on and making out he was
Scott calling Dug out. Neal said Dug come out of the
room all piss-eyed and fucked up on downers, waving a
cutlass and a broken golf club, bare chested and roaring
in dirty jeans and boots, his black hair tied in little plaits.
He'd put burning kitchen matches in his plaits, Neal
said. Scott and Neal jumped him when he came out the
room. The boys kicked and punched him until he was
down. They stamped on his head until the little flames
in his hair blew out. There was blood up the walls, Neal
said, blood on their boots and Levi's. I know, I said, I
saw it.

You know how long you were in there? Neal said,
and when I didn't answer he said two nights and a day.
You should have seen your brother, he said.

All wet with blood Scott and Neal called out to Tony
Angelino and Al Babe and Eddie and they came in
through the doors and windows, all pop eyed and
shaven headed like the vengeful midnight ghosts of
ruined boys from Dug's dreams. They burned Dug with
cigarette ends. Scott went out to the yard and came back
with a jerry can of petrol and splashed some petrol over
Dug and set him on fire. They let him burn and then
they all pissed on him. They stripped him and Eddie got
a beer bottle and stuck it up him. Neal said he thought
Scott would stop Eddie then but Scott didn't. Go on,
Eddie, Scott said, stick it up his fucking arse. He was
right out there, Neal said, Scott, and Neal didn't know if
he was ever coming back. After that Dug lay on the floor
and Scott kept kicking him in the head and laughing
until Neal had to get a hold of Scott to stop him. They
dragged Dug out and kicked him down the stairs and
out into the yard. They put him in the back of one of his
cars and drove him up out of town and threw him out of
the car at the top of Paradise Woods like a beaten dog

you didn't want and never wanted anybody to ever find.

"And nothing's been heard of him since?" I said.

"Nothing's been heard of him Horse."

After he'd told me, Neal smoked a cigarette and looked at me sideways like he didn't want me to see him looking because then I'd know how he felt about me now. It was how he looked at Eddie Beer after Eddie went out and got his face tattooed. Neal looked at Eddie, and he looked at me now, like he couldn't believe we had let these things happen to us. He could feel for you, Neal could, but he couldn't see past what Dug had done to me being my own fault. He wasn't on his own there.

Deep down though Neal was good hearted. He didn't want me to know that was how he felt. I used to look for it though, and whenever I saw him Neal couldn't keep that look off his face for long. I had the feeling that it was all he could do not to kick the shit out of me for letting Scott and him down. Besides Eddie and Steve Tardelli and Taylor Beaumont, that's how everybody was with me. I was sick of it but I understood it. I was still a boy and it was how I felt about me. So you can bet that even before he was taken away I tried to stay away from Scott.

Years later I remembered Neal saying that if you didn't man up you got fucked up the arse. That was what life was. I remembered him saying that and I remember thinking well, I did man up and I still got fucked up the arse. So, in different but no less permanent ways, did Neal and Scott and all the others. So what does that tell you?

The thing is nothing happened straightaway. I mean the police didn't come and Dug didn't come riding back into town, not then and not ever. Still I guess everybody must have been waiting to be picked up. Scott was, I think, though it was hard for me to tell. I was mostly just out of it. Eddie had found all of Dug's Mandys and DS118s when the skinheads were going through the place and he shared them with me. Eddie said not to tell anybody where I'd got them but I wasn't talking much

at all then. I was just closed down. I'd wake up in the
late morning some time and smoke a joint and take a pill
and that would be me monged and spinning out. Taylor
Beaumont used to come round sometimes and take me
for a walk on the beach and try to talk to me but it didn't
really matter to me where I was or what was happening.
So I asked Neal to put it all together for me afterwards
when Scott had been picked up and I'd run out of pills
for a little while. It was all just information though. I still
wasn't close to feeling anything.

When the days went by into September and the
police still didn't come and there was nothing heard
from Dug, Neal told me that Scott began to get loose.
Except for the downers Eddie managed to get, and that
he didn't know about, Scott had kept everything they'd
found up at Dug's for himself and he was acting like a
big man with it in the Wagon. He'd get high and when
he was tranced he'd go on and on about going to
Morocco or India like his friend Coop. Somewhere hot.
Anywhere hot but he didn't go. People started drifting
away. They didn't want to be with him. Gary Angelino
started serving up out of his rooms at the Spartan down
by Langney Point and I guess the boys could see what
was coming and went with Gaz.

At the finish Neal said, it was just me and your
brother and Julie Spanish in there, don't believe what
anybody else tells you. I mean Uptown kids would come
in to score still, Neal said, but nobody stuck around, and
after a while everybody went over to Gary. I think a lot
of people came into the Wagon just to say they had, if
you know what I mean. It was like that in there. You
never knew when your brother was going to mouth off
at you or throw a bottle or beat the shit out of you. Neal
said the one thing everybody who went in there knew
was not to talk about you. Anybody said anything to
him about you and Scott went mental. Your mate Taylor
came in asking after you and Scott was about to rip his
head off before I stepped in. That's all it took for
everything to go bad Neal said, looking at me sideways,

just a couple of weeks at the end of the summer.

I stayed away from Scott like I say, because I believed he'd have looked at me the way Neal did, and tell me what I took all the Mandys not to hear. I thought he was mad at me. Mad at me for me going round there on my own I mean. I don't know that there's a word for how Scott felt about what Dug did to me before he got there and for what he had to do to get me out. Sitting on the beach the night it happened, with the smell of the burning car close by, he said, "I don't know if it's ever going to get any better Kim, but you got to believe it will," and although I know he was talking to me sometimes I think he was talking to himself. Scott wasn't stupid. He could see what was coming for both of us, and I know he loved me but he was ashamed of me too, so now that was a fight we were both having with ourselves.

Scott expected to get locked up sometime like most of the boys I knew and because he was Scott there were stories about how he went because how you went was a big thing, and travelled with you wherever they took you.

It was the Maltese, Neal said. There was never a word said about Dug. It's like that night never happened. It was all the stuff that went on in the Wagon, the Rocky and all of that, so it must have been the Maltese. What, George? I said. Yeah, Neal said, he disappeared at the end of August and the police came for me and Scott in the second week of September on the last hot day of the year, so work it out for yourself. We were on our own in the Wagon, Neal said, and they just walked me and your brother out of there. Why didn't they put you away? I said. Scott took it all on himself, Neal said. That was a big thing for him to do. Scott hadn't been inside before and he knew they'd lock me up for a long time. I owe him big time. They put Scott in Rochester, which Neal said was a tough place. I was up there last week, he said. He's grown his hair. He's still tough though. He doesn't understand why you won't

171

visit him, I don't either.

"I just can't."

"I don't get it."

"I know, you said."

Eddie Beer told me Scott cut up rough and fought the police all the way to the car they took him away in. Eddie said it took four or five big police to put Scott in the car and he still broke his way out and legged it up the road and the police had to chase him down. Scott was laughing, Eddie said.

Eddie said skinheads came out of the Wagon and the Regal and started fighting the police up and down Seaside Road. The boys fighting for Scott this last time. Scott's brick red face and sun lightened crop becoming dark as the last of the summer sun went down behind the Regal Arcade and the Painted Wagon. Scott finally disappearing under the black forms who swarmed over him.

I heard what Neal told me but I wanted to believe what Eddie said. The way Eddie told the stories reminded me of when I was younger and I had told stories about Scott to make myself feel better. I told Neal what Eddie had said and he said to me, who you going to believe, me or stone mad Eddie Beer?

Years later I asked Julie Spanish about it. Taylor Beaumont helped me find her. They'd put her in a two up, two down council house way out in the east of town near Langney Point. Julie was bringing up two boys on her own by then but you could see in her eyes that my brother was still real to her. Julie was wide-eyed looking at my tattoos. We stood in the small front garden while Julie smoked a cigarette because she wouldn't smoke in the house. She said she just looked around and Scott was gone.

"How do you mean?"

"You don't think things will ever change when you're young," she said. "Scott was so big to me. He just filled my world, and when he went it was like the sea not being there you know?"

I said that I did. Julie was tan and she wore cut-offs and a cheesecloth shirt. Her black hair fell straight down her back, and smelled like green apples.

"Did he write to you from there?" I said.

"Not from there. I got some postcards from him, afterwards."

There was a red trike fallen sideways on the brown grass, and a beat up green Hulk standing over an action man with no head. Julie stood with the sun in her eyes remembering the boy she loved when she was young. You could hear her sons fighting in the little house.

THAT'S HOW my star fell and everything went dark. I used to believe, in those first years after Dug raped me, that it would have been better if my story had ended the same way as Johnny Cade's. I had nothing to trade, no kids to save from burning fires, but I could see no way to be the hero of my own life except to end it. Nobody was ever charged over Dug. It was like it never happened, like Neal said, except that Dug was always there in my dreams, him and the kid whose face I broke. I did hear a story that Dug died on his motorbike going over the high side when he was coming back from the Bulldog Bash in the late summer of 1989, but even so he still comes for me at night, riding into my sleep on bloody horses like the ones I'd seen fingerpainted on Eddie Beer's jeans. Dug with fire in his hair and pushing his fat cock at me. People say that you can't dream your own death but I used to do it all the time. There was no decisive act in me though, one way or another, and so without wanting to or knowing why, I held on.

After Scott went to prison there were no skinheads left except for me and Eddie Beer and we didn't count. I never saw Dawn again. Boys were left to find their own way and some of them didn't make it. Al Babe turned into the walking dead, living on the beach and robbing the white hotels for drug money, and they found him dead one morning in a shelter by the bandstand under the memorial for John Wesley Woodward. Knowing that Al Babe had been up in the school on the downs before me I wonder if I wasn't the only one who couldn't always separate Dug and Anderson in my mind. I remembered how lovely Al Babe's sea coloured eyes had been. I did hear that somebody tried to get Anderson locked up but that he had got out of it somehow and was back teaching in another school. That used to burn me up. The Persians started calling themselves mujahideen and talking about revolution and going home. Scott was in prison for two years.

I had to get away. People in the town were talking about me and about Scott and I couldn't stand it. I ran away to London and spent some time sleeping rough until I moved into a squat in Vauxhall. I met lots of boys like me on the streets. In London I saw boys and men fighting all the time; in the parks and underpasses where I tried to sleep at night; on the building sites where I sometimes found work as a day labourer; in little roads south of the river at closing time outside the pubs where I pissed away the money it had been so hard to earn. Sometimes I found myself right in it, throwing and taking punches and kicks. People started carrying weapons. I saw people stabbed. The first time I heard a gunshot was at a dance in Somerleyton Road, in Brixton. I kept my head cropped down. New cuts and scars joined the old ones. My hands and face grew thick. Time passed in this blind way, two years, then three, four, five.

Scott got out of prison and went to India at last. I didn't see him when he got out or before he left. I kept away from him. He stayed in India for a long time and travelled all over that country, from Chennai to Amritsar. He got high with the Sadhus at Khumba Mela in Allahabad. He crossed the border, and from Peshawar he disappeared into the mountain territory between Pakistan and Afghanistan. After a year he turned up in Australia where he ran a marathon in Sydney and another one in Melbourne. He went from Australia into Sarawak and from there into Cambodia and Laos. I heard he trained as a Muy Thai boxer and was living and fighting in Bangkok for a while, and then maybe he had a girl down in the islands in the south of Thailand for a year or two. He went on into other countries and you would sometimes not hear from him for months. My brother seemed to travel lightly, always in the ever present, and I believed then that he did not carry with him the things that had happened before. I imagined that Scott had come fully into himself in these long years of wandering, completely tough but not angry anymore,

175

walking in his own path at last. He sent me little postcards from all over and I never answered them and they kept coming. When I thought about my brother, and I thought about him all the time, I thought about him being *out there* at last, and I tried to hope that out there was everything he had dreamed it would be. The plain fact though is that back then I had come to hate him for where I'd thought he left me: out of my mind and raging and still tasting Dug's sour cock in my mouth whenever I closed my eyes and tried to sleep.

I hadn't been in London much more than a year when I heard that Eddie Beer had jumped in front of a train. It hit me hard about Eddie, when I got to where I could feel things again. Maybe you saw it coming reading this, like in *The Outsiders* when you know straight off Johnny Cade won't make it to the end of the book. It's different in real life though, how it makes you feel. Still, boys like Johnny Cade and Eddie Beer, you couldn't give them a happy ending.

Most of the things I knew about home I heard from Steve Tardelli and Taylor Beaumont. At the time I thought it was just one of those things, running into Taylor in London, but I'm not so sure now he wasn't looking for me. You do find out who your friends are and that's the truth. I think maybe Steve sent him. Steve sent me little postcards too.

It was a late afternoon in early autumn I remember. I had just finished some cash in hand day labouring with an Irish roadwork gang, men from Skibereen mostly, and I was drinking two-handed with them in a squatters pub called the Royal Oak in Vauxhall, not understanding much of what was being said, and fast spending all the money I had earned that day. I had a girlfriend then and in that part of my heart that was never drunk I knew that I should go home, while the autumn sunlight was still streaming in through the window, and while I still had some money left in my pocket to give her. The squat I was staying in was close by the pub and the girl I was with then, a pale long-haired girl called Robin, was waiting for me there. Robin was from a nice family in the country. She had come to London to be a painter and she was looking inside herself for any wildness she might have. We drank all the time. Robin drank because she liked to but she also drank because she loved me. I made her love me and I fucked her over again and again. I never did tell her the truth. Not her or anybody else until I met my wife. Araba.

I had given up trying to follow the conversation and I was watching a fight on the TV when Taylor came in. I watched him come through the bar. He looked the same as the last time I'd seen him, like rock and roll hadn't died, all blond quiff and Buddy Holly glasses and Chukka shoes. I was dressed the same as the Irishmen in dirty jeans and T-shirt and work boots and one of those sleeveless flourescent jackets and it took a while before Taylor saw me. A black haired Irishman with tan arms and a red face started singing *Carrickfergus*. It's not just the beer that's flat then, Taylor said when he sat down.

I asked about people, and Taylor told me the stories I'm telling you. Later he went through all the dead people we knew. That's kind of Taylor's thing. He's strong on where we come from and what all the stories mean. There's Eddie and Al Babe and Donnie Orange, and there were some others where Taylor had to remind me who they were.

Afterwards, when I was sitting up late while Robin slept, and drinking lager and smoking skunkweed in the dark, I remembered hearing how little Gary Angelino had gone over Beachy Head when he was eighteen or so. I don't know if he jumped or if he fell. I heard he had a girl up there and when he came out of her he fell. Like I say Taylor knows all the stories so you'd have to ask him. I just know bits and pieces. It was seeing Taylor again that really started me thinking about Scott and why we did the things we did and turned out this way, and everything I'm telling you now.

I saw Taylor once or twice a month after that. He was

living in another squat, in Kennington. I'll be honest and
say there's a whole bunch of time I don't remember. I
still thought that what had happened to me was written
on me for people to read and I didn't like it when
anybody looked at me. I went about trying to shut all
that out the way I always had, by drinking and drugging
for England. I was punchy and I had blackouts all the
time. One night I'd been drinking and somewhere along
the way home I got beaten up again but badly this time.
I don't remember what happened, nothing. Just coming
round in my room. Blood on the floor and broken ribs
and my girlfriend Robin crying in the corner, her straw
blonde hair hanging down her back like a rope in the
sun, the smell of her sized canvasses strong in the room.
We couldn't make it after that.

Like I say Taylor had no time for violence of any
kind. I remember sitting on the floor of his room in
Kennington, drinking tea and listening to Taylor's
Johnny Burnette and Sleepy LaBeef records, my face
swollen and my ribs taped. Some hip-hop djs had taken
over the house next door and Taylor's old scratchy
records clashed with the Public Enemy beats coming
through the walls. Taylor made pots of tea and listened
to me while I went on. He was wearing a white Hanes T-
shirt stretched tight over his stomach, and taped high on
his thick right arm there was a white guaze pad with
some blood showing through. I didn't know what it was
and didn't ask. When Taylor looked at me through his
big black glasses his blurred green eyes were magnified
and googly.

"Kim, you're the only one who can stop this
happening otherwise you're not going to make it. And
nobody will really give a shit except for maybe me and
Steve and your brother. Has anything you've done made
you feel better about yourself?"

"No," I said.

"Well then you've got to get off all this self-
destruction bollocks and find something to believe in."

"What," I said, "like rock and roll?"

"Hey," Taylor said, "don't knock the rock. I'm thinking of getting one of those answerphones in here. Press one for the money, two for the show."

A little while after Robin left me I started swimming again just to get the sight of Dug standing over me out of my head. I swam, slowly and not everyday at first, in south London's outside pools at Tooting and Brockwell Park. Scott wrote me from out of the blue that winter, from Nepal I think. He said that he was into real long swims now and there was one in the Himalayas that he had heard about, some twenty mile river swim that a bunch of people did every year in wet suits with snow falling, and maybe he would get into that. Why not just get it together?

I think about Scott staying away but keeping fragile contact all those years from all over with no answer from me. I think about the care he must have taken and how he must have looked up from his life and thought of me. What skies he sat under to write them. How far he must have walked sometimes, coming down from some cloud-circled mountain to get them posted. All the cards begin the same way. All right Kim, are you OK? And then he'd tell me about some fantastic place in the high mountains or an empty golden beach and I would see him skylined against the fire bright sun, happy, in shorts forever, and then the anger would kick in and I couldn't read anymore. It's only now when I find and read again one of these old cards that's been keeping my place in a book that I see how much he really wanted to know the answer to his question. Back then, when they came, I hardly read them at all. I guess by never writing back I told my brother what he needed to know about me, and the cards kept coming.

What happened to Neal in the end, well, I don't know what you'd make of it. Taylor said Neal stayed home roofing and that had aged him. With the boys who died, and the boys who went away, I guess there were only a few people left who remembered that Neal had been Bombhead. Taylor was one of them and Neal used to talk to him when he saw him out in the town. Neal talked about your brother all the time, Taylor told me, and the wild things they had done together when they were young.

Some men can carry the loss of their boyhood lightly I've found, and some of us do not.

I don't remember why but Taylor Beaumont had always had a thing about Galley Mouratidis, the beach girl Al Babe was seeing that summer. When they were little Taylor and Galley lived close by each other. Galley grew up wild, with this long swimmer's high-hipped frame, and I think Taylor put himself on standby when she got in trouble and needed him. Anyway Neal started going with her and they got married. The story was that Neal was crazy about Galley but that she ran around. Taylor believed that Neal took Galley's running around as a judgement on the colour of his skin, and that this told you more about Neal than it did about Galley. About how and where Neal had grown up.

I thought that Neal's life had taught him that you had to fight to stop being fucked. He had let down the hard mask to love Galley and when she cheated on him beating on her was the only answer he had to how that made him feel, and yes, I know it wasn't the right one. It's just that I knew Neal and had been close to him at one time in my life. I thought I could understand his heart. Besides, I know how hard it is to unlearn the patterns of your life that will destroy you if you let them. More than hard, if you want to know the truth. From a boy you get locked into a way of being where blood is the only answer and it can take you all your life to grow away from that. Maybe if he had gone away with Scott and seen the things my brother had, then Neal would have learned different, but he didn't, and he beat his wife and it was wrong. Mostly Galley ran to Taylor afterwards and Taylor always took her in. Taylor patched her up and looked after her until in the end she stayed. I knew what would happen next, Taylor said.

Neal came for Taylor in the Ocean Wave. He drove

his car into the pub. I knew that I'd have to take a beating Taylor said, and I did. When I came round he was stuffing all the love poems I'd written her into my mouth. I couldn't get anything else out of Taylor but the point is Neal spun out after that and lost himself in the cheap heroin that was flooding through the town and chased it with hash and sweet wine, and was found washed up on the beach under the Pier on a dark morning in late October. That's all mine to carry around now, Taylor said. Him and Galley weren't together anymore, and now Taylor was in London. Somebody once said that for your life to be worth anything sooner or later you must know terrible regret, Taylor said, and you must face it down or your life will be ruined. Are you talking to me, I said. I'm just saying, Taylor said, you aren't the only one.

One night round at Taylor's and listening to *Fight the Power* coming through the walls like thunder, I asked him about Steve Tardelli.

Taylor told me that Steve had stayed home beachcombing in the winters and travelling around Sussex in the summers with a fair.

"What was he doing there?"

"Learning to tattoo," Taylor said. He said that Steve had apprenticed himself to an old tattooist called Stoney who travelled with the fair and worked out of a shop in Hastings in the winter.

A few months later when Taylor asked me to come down and help him and Steve clean out and decorate a shop Steve had rented and that he was going to tattoo out of, I found myself saying yes because there was no real reason to say no. In the second week of May I went home for the first time in eight years, travelling down on my own a night after I said I would, because I got drunk and high the day before.

IN THOSE days there was a compartment at the front of the train that looked like a first class carriage but wasn't, and I sat in there with the door closed and the window open, smoking and drinking beer that had been cold when I bought it from the station in London but that became warm as the train went south. Soon after we left the city we passed the lights of the airport from where Scott had flown to distant shores, to blue seas and high mountains. The night became dark as I travelled until the world outside disappeared and only my face came back at me from the window.

I walked out to the violet, star filled southern night to meet Taylor. His blond hair was cut down to a Mac Curtis flat top so that he looked younger, and later Taylor told me he had been to Fred's in Brighton on his way down from London. He was waiting for me by the benches outside the train station where three men were drinking and talking to the air. There was a young girl with them wearing dirty white shoes, and she was dancing and drinking something out of a big brown plastic bottle.

The town was like the beach after the tide goes out. It looked the same but it had changed. I don't know what I expected. It seemed smaller, the way everybody says places are when you go back to them. I guess I thought the town would still be full of gangs of boys fighting and that everybody would know me and what had happened. But the summer when my brother had been king of the skinheads and I had been held prisoner and raped was yesterday only to me, and the one tribe I could see were a bunch of long -haired skater kids wearing Quicksilver and Fat Face and riding boards and they didn't look like much. Still, the skater kids reminded me of Gary Angelino, and there were ghosts on every corner.

We went to Steve's early the next morning. The shop was at the top of a three-floor stand-alone building on a side street just up from the beach. On the other floors were a recording studio and performance space. There was an iron staircase outside that went up to a little landing and the door to the shop, and going up the stairs we could hear the rockabilly Steve was playing loud. When my boots chimed on the stairs I flashed on Al Babe walking on the iron fire escape to Dug's rooms but the bad feeling came and went straightaway. I was good at closing myself down.

There was a bell that rang and we came into a high-ceilinged room flooded with sunlight from a big picture window that looked out to the sea. To the right was an empty doorway through to a smaller room that was also sun lightened. There was another doorway in the left hand corner that went through to a small kitchen. The walls were stripped and unpainted. The floor was bare and the boards were dirty. There was a big wooden counter like a bar in front of you when you came in the door. Steve was up a step-ladder whitewashing the ceiling and the light fell on him. There were spots of paint on the floorboards. There was a De Walt toolbox open on the floor by the ladder, and round and about there were five litre tins of paint and rolls of differently graded sandpaper. Steve had a series of mantras tattooed on his back over rocks and flowers and falling water, and as he reached to paint the muscles in his back popped and moved and the mantras seemed to skip and buck over the tattooed waves.

Steve's shelf of hair was cropped down to a white grey flat top. But for those big ears he was kind of stripped down generally, all knotty muscle and thick ropy veins. His drawn and lined face seemed carved out of wood like a Tiki head; his nose sharp as an axe blade. He was slim-hipped and wearing old, low waister Lee jeans that had white paint splashes on them, and paper Japanese slippers and nothing else. He had three-quarter length tattooed sleeves with black grey whirlwinds at the elbows and scalloped edged chest panels of waves and flowers. Steve came down the ladder and turned

183

down the tape player. He hugged me and kissed me on the forehead.

"You found him," he said to Taylor.

"I always get my man."

"Mate," Steve said, "it's been a while. Must be seven or eight years."

"It must be," I said.

"You ready for a day's work?" Steve said to me.

"If Taylor ever gets the kettle on," I said.

That weekend we finished painting all the walls white and when the paint was dry we sanded and varnished the floors. At the top of the wall that divided the main part of the studio from the smaller room Steve was going to tattoo in, there were maybe a dozen glass panes, and Steve had made Sanskrit character stencils and put one in the centre of each piece of glass to spell out what he said was a strong mantra. Early Sunday morning me and Steve put up some Tibetan prayer flags outside that are still there, sun and wind faded now and heavy with salt.

On Sunday night we drank cold beer and had some Chinese food and I listened to Taylor and Steve talk about tattooing. Steve believed in the magic power of tattoos, that's how he felt about it.

"Magic how?" I said to him, as Taylor opened cartons of food and popped the tops off bottles of Tiger beer. There were floating frames full of tattoo postcards, shop cards, sheets of old flash designs, Steve's own flash stacked against all the walls. There were individual photographs set in frames: tattooed Berber women, a sheet of Iban designs and another of Marquesan tattoos, a large print of Joshua Reynolds' painting of the tattooed Tahitian Omai. There were piles of tattoo books on the floor. We sat on large, old, bleached out pieces of driftwood that Steve had smoothed out for the purpose.

Pink-red light came in the windows and blazed in the Sanskrit letters set in the glass panes. There were people walking on the seafront in the last light of the day. Steve was wearing a Jack Rudy T-shirt and his old Lees, and he sat with a bowl of stir-fry noodles in his lap and talked.

"You can't find a place in the world where the people didn't tattoo or mark themselves in some way," Steve said. "They might have had it civilised out of them for a hundred years or so but it always comes back, and there are as many reasons people give for tattooing as there are tattoos. Some places in India you can't get to heaven unless you have the right tattoos, and there were tribes in Africa who went in for heavy tattooing and scarring to make themselves worthless to slave traders. There are tattoos for fertility, tattoos to protect women during pregnancy. Then you've got tattoos like this," Steve showed me a page of Iban designs, "these Borneo stars here that you'd get when you'd taken a head. Same thing in the Himalayas with the Naga people there or young Bushmen in Africa who kill their first antelope and then get tattooed. A lot of tattoos are about that, coming into yourself, marking a change. And it hurts of course, that's part of all that."

Taylor laughed. "It fucking hurts," he said, "don't be lying to Kim now."

Taylor sat with his shirt off and I could see that he had a large Hammer and Sickle tattooed on one side of his chest and a Sacred Heart on the other. I didn't think I'd ever seen Taylor without a shirt on. He had some above-the-elbow line and shading work on his arms where Steve had started working on his sleeves. On the top of his left shoulder he had an old tattoo of the little cartoon dog Droopy, roughly drawn and fading on the skin.

"I know it hurts," I said

"But did you ever think about it?" Steve said. "Look at this."

He put his bowl on the floor and went to a corner of the room and picked out a framed picture and brought it over and handed it to me. It was a large, old, black and white photograph of a Maori man who was looking into the camera with fierce staring black eyes. His thin mouth was set in a downward curve and his bottom lip stuck out very slightly. His hair was grey and high on his forehead and long over his ears. His face was tattooed with dark symmetrical spirals and arcs, and beyond the beauty of the patterns what you could see most plainly was how deeply the cuts of the tattoo went into the skin. You could have made the sharp end of a pencil disappear in the grooves of his face.

"Each of these mokos is unique," Steve said. "This one tells this man's story, his rank, his ancestors, his battle honours. The thing that gets me though, every time I look at one of these, is how far it's bashed into his face. The tattooist would have a tool, made from stick or bone, with teeth on the end, anywhere from a few teeth to sixty or so. They dipped the stick in a kind of ink made from tree ash, bird fat and dog shit, pricked the skin with that and then they'd hammer the stick with a bigger stick or a kind of mallet. I don't know how people sat still for that, except to say that taking it was a big part of it. This man would be admired for what the moko told about him, but also because he had it at all. You proved your bravery getting this on, not just to the people in your tribe but to yourself."

Steve stood up and took the picture back to the wall. He sat down and looked at the pale pink, floating cherry blossom petals and black shading tattooed on the inside of his right arm.

"You can't run from the pain when you're getting tattooed." He said. "You got to face it head on. You can take it inside yourself, talk to it, but you can't run from it. Maybe the pain gets mixed in with other shit that's happened to you, where the pain has just sat there for years and you've poured lager on it or thrown pills at it or whatever and nothing works. Some people find that when the tattoo pain has gone the other stuff's gone too."

"How's that work?" I said. "They're different things." I was tired and hot in my face and angry at all the talking. I opened another beer. I'd left a lot of food in my

186

bowl. Steve didn't seem to notice that I was angry but he reached over and took my bowl and ate the food I'd left.

"It works because if the tattoo is beautiful and maybe because you've always wanted it there's at least one part of you, the tattooed part, that you're not going to hate anymore. And when you look at the tattoo you feel good. So the pain is mixed in somehow with something good, not just everything that's bad."

I lit a cigarette to go with the beer.

"What about magic?" I said.

Steve got out some rolling tobacco and papers and made a cigarette.

"Say you're a fisherman in ten hundred and something and living in Van Lang in South Asia, Land of the Tattooed People. You get tattoos of sea monsters, snakes, crocodiles and what have you to protect you from getting killed by these animals out at sea. All that kind of tattooing is strong in Asia, in Burma and Thailand, Laos, Cambodia. You go to Thailand now and the monks out there will still tattoo you with magic formulas and signs. It's a big tourist thing as well as a living tradition. Protect you from snakes, bullets, and swords, getting sacked from your job or dumped by your girlfriend. If you don't drown or get eaten or get dumped or whatever, the tattoos are magic. If shit does happen then you didn't observe all the rituals properly before you were tattooed so it's your fault not the tattoos."

"So it's bullshit." I said.

"No," said Steve, "I don't think it is bullshit. What's important is how you feel about it. If you think your tattoos are magic and beautiful you're going to feel protected and beautiful, especially if you didn't before. You're going to feel strong remembering the pain, how you took it, and you might not be scared of pain again. You been tattooed on the face for six hours you might think you'll be able to deal with what might have hurt you in the past and anything else that comes your way. I'm talking about if you're tattooed, there's a difference between having a tattoo and being tattooed. If you believe your tattoos protect you from sea monsters you're going to do your job well. Old time Japanese fire-fighters used to have all these warriors tattooed on them, help them be brave enough to put out fires."

"Tattoo power," said Taylor. He was still sitting shirtless on the driftwood seat. His belly spilled out over his vintage jeans.

"You buy into this too?" I said.

Taylor took a pull of beer and lit a cigarette.

"Mate," he said, "All my life I've hated taking my shirt off. Go to bed with the light off, all that. Hated the bloody sight of myself. Don't now."

"I didn't know that," I said.

"You never asked. It doesn't matter. Self-hatred, where would we be without it? Steve would be out of bloody work."

"What about if you get *Fuck the World* put on you, crazy stuff like that, *Straight to Hell*?" I said.

"Like that mate of yours who jumped in front of a train? The one with the swastika and lightning bolts on his face?" Steve said.

"Eddie, Eddie Beer."

"You think the tattoos he had made him feel better about himself?"

When I didn't answer Steve said, "Lots of people get hard nut tattoos. If you're a boy that's the first thing you think of. You get Death Heads or *Born to Lose* or *Love and Hate*. You know what it's like Kim, some boys need to feel tough. That kind of stuff can put you in a bad place for sure, carrying all that bad ink around. It's pretty straightforward. Law of Karma."

"I knew somebody had 1% tattooed on his hand. Do you know what that means?"

"That's a Hells Angels thing isn't it Taylor?" Steve said.

Taylor said, "It means we're the 1% who don't fit in and who don't care. He wasn't an Angel though was he?"

"He was but then they kicked him out when they found out about him. He had *AFFA* on him too."

"*Angels Forever, Forever Angels.*" Taylor said.

"Who we talking about?" said Steve.

The sun was starting to fall in the afternoon and the light in the room was soft. The windows were open. The air was sea sweet and mixed in with the smell of new paint. In the moments when the gulls were quiet I could hear the sea. Taylor looked at me like he didn't know what I was going to say but whatever it was would be fine with him. I looked at Steve, tender and sure and quiet, and across the room at the man in the picture with the beautiful tattooed face. I laughed suddenly. The sound of it surprised me.

"Fuck," I said. "Nobody."

The light continued to fade until we were sat in near darkness. Steve put a dub tape on low and I think we all tuned out to separate places for a little while, our thoughts folding into, and arranging, themselves. All I can say for certain is that it got quiet.

"What about us?" I said after a time. "What's our history? We're not from Borneo or the Himalayas."

"Well," Steve said, "How many people do you know with tattoos? In this town when you were living here?"

I remembered the bucket of blood shop up by Fusciardi's and the tattoo parlour on the Pier. I told Steve all the boys I knew were crazy for tattoos: Scott and Bombhead, Eddie Beer.

Steve said, "And all those old boys on the seafront with navy tattoos. I bet you every town in England has a tattooist. Every seaside town definitely. For us, especially coming up here, tattooing has this connection with the sea, and that's the stuff I'm really into following up. All the sailors that went out from places like this brought back tattoos from all over, from the Marquesan Islands, Tahiti, Hawaii, and they had their own magic tattoos. A sailor would have a shipwreck put on him, a *Sailor's Grave*, to protect him from shipwrecks. He'd have a pig and a rooster put on his feet to keep him from

189

drowning, turnscrews to get him to shore if he was washed overboard."

Taylor was over by the window. "Hey," he said, "look at that."

Steve and I went over to the window. I hadn't looked at the southern sky for a long time. It was just before dark, and the sky swept away with no end over the sea towards Pevensey Bay and Hastings and held, it seemed to me, all the shapes and colours that I had seen in Taylor and Steve's tattoos and in the tattoo books and pictures Steve had shown me. The pink-red blushed floating clouds were heaped and fluffed like the clouds on Steve's shoulders, and their colour was the colour of the cherry blossom tattooed on his arms. The sun was going down behind the clouds and firing out jets of orange light. The moon was yet to rise, and the sea had turned to deep, soft velvet black like the ink in the whirlwinds on Steve's elbows.

"That's nice," Steve said.

Taylor said, "You know how they identified the body of King Harold after the Battle of Hastings? He had the name of his country and his wife tattooed on his chest."

I STARTED coming down at weekends to help Steve out,
working in the shop until the late warm afternoons
before going down to the beach with Steve. I began to
find myself again in the cold water and under the
southern sun. Steve started putting work on me. We'd
come back from the beach and have a cold beer. I'd
shower in the little bathroom he had there and when the
sun bloom had settled down in my skin in the evening
Steve would say, do you want a bit on then? Mostly I
went for good luck charms: prayers and mantras in
Sanskrit, and sea tattoos, anchors and waves, nautical
stars and a *Sailor's Grave* because the sea was where I
came from. I had pretty, blue hibiscus flowers tattooed
on my feet.

I tried to sit with the pain like Steve said. I'd close my
eyes and the different kinds of pain, the slow sharp deep
burn of the outliner, or the hot raw drag of the shader
say, were different colours behind my closed eyes. I was
fighting the pain though, was the truth, and Steve could
tell and said not to, it would make it harder, so then I
tried to take it in and accept it. I tried to surf the pain,
riding on top of it as lightly as I could until sometimes, if
I had slept the night before and was not drinking or
drugging too hard, I got so how I could leave Steve and
my body and the tattoo machine and the pain behind
and go into different spaces and times.

Steve had an old desk stuffed with stencils and
drawings and thank you cards and letters from people
he had tattooed. Above the workbench where he kept
his gloves, tape, gauze pads, inks, machines, needles,
and autoclave he had a small framed picture next to a
copper incense holder on a little narrow wooden shelf.
The incense holder was full of ashes and some ashes had
spilled out on to the shelf. Steve said that the picture was
of a Vietnamese monk called Thich Nhat Hanh. Below
the picture were printed the words: If we are peaceful, if

we are happy, we can smile, and everyone in our family, our entire society will benefit from our peace.

Were Steve and Taylor right about what they said? I don't know, they knew more about it than I did and I can only speak for me. Mostly I felt energised after being tattooed and connected to life in a way that I had not felt for a long time. I mean I could take pleasure in feeling the sun on me. Sometimes, when Steve had stopped working on me, I would feel a strange sweet absence, as if the pain that had stopped was not just the pain of being tattooed. It did not often last for more than a day at first, this lightness, but I learnt to recognise it when it happened and try to keep it going, like a new and fragile fire in my heart. I learnt to look forward to being tattooed.

I told Steve about it once, after he'd put a red and black nautical star on my ribs, and he said yes it could do that. I said it was like when I was a kid and went sea swimming in the spring when the water was really cold. Some days when I was a little kid I'd feel fluttery and all locked out of myself for no reason at all that I could name. I guess that's when I first learnt about swimming. I'd go down to the beach and swim in the cold water. I'd have to gee myself up to get in and it hurt, the water, when it was that cold, but afterwards I'd have a buzz on and would feel like myself again, gentle and connected to the world and to its true possibilities. It's been a long time since I felt like that, I said.

"What happened to you is part of you Kim," Steve said. "I know you think everybody can see it on you all the time. Maybe when people look at you now they see something else, these finger waves or flowers, maybe this star."

"I don't know", I said, "I suppose what it is for me is I look at this flower here on my arm and although I say I remember how much it hurt to get it, when you put it on, I can't really remember and it doesn't hurt now. What's left is the flower. Same as what happened to me hurt me. It nearly killed me to have that happen but I'm still here."

Steve put his needles in the autoclave on his workbench, threw his gloves into the bin, and wiped down his surfaces.

"There you go," he said, "You want a cold beer?"

Tony Angelino came into the shop one June day when I was there. Tony, gone all big with beer and weights and wearing a wife beater. He was starting to get an early summer tan on, his big shoulders and arms were coming in dark and golden but he was still mostly real deep red over his chest, like all the blood was gathered and pooling under there. I hadn't seen him in years. I didn't know how he'd be with me but when he recognised me he hugged me and called me Horse and nobody had done that for years. He didn't look at me the way I thought he would. He asked after Scott but I couldn't tell him much, and said I only knew that Scott was trekking somewhere in South America. Steve had made up a stencil from a photograph of Gary that Tony had brought in. In the picture Gary was tan and his long, fair skaters hair was pushed back out of his sleepy blue eyes. Steve put it on over Tony's heart in fine line, single needle, grey black ink, Gary's face and memory slowly revealed over his brother's heart. It took Steve all afternoon, and underneath he put Gary's name and his dates. Next to the new tattoo Tony's old skinhead tats looked faded and old.

I watched Steve work as the light in the studio changed and moved. I made Tony and Steve cups of tea and when people came in I showed them folders with Steve's flash and custom work in and made bookings. Steve tattooed while Tony talked about Gary. The two men had their heads close together and I couldn't hear what Tony was saying over the buzzing of the machine. When the piece was finished and Steve had put a gauze pad on it to stop the blood, Tony's face had just softened right down and you could see what he had looked like when he was a kid. "I've been meaning to do that for a long time," he said. "Fuck it's sore though."

When Tony was leaving he said goodbye to me.

I hugged him and said, "I don't think I've ever thanked you Tone, for back then."

"Mate," he said, "it's not me you should be thanking. I don't know how things stand between you and Scott but I can guess if you don't know where he is. If you need to make peace you need to do it now, before it's too late. When you see him say hello from me Kim, all right. Tell him Ange sends his love."

I promised Tony that I would, and late that night it really came to me that Neal, Al Babe, Eddie Beer, and Gary Angelino were dead and gone forever, and that they were boys who had come to save me. Tony Angelino and my brother were still alive but I didn't know where Tony lived, and I still couldn't fill one of Scott's little postcards with what I knew about him.

I AM made by all the boys and men I knew and by the particular arrangement of light and water under southern skies. Configured like the beaches I grew up on by the permanent heavy music and movement of deep water. Now, and for the last few years, I am shaped by my wife Araba and by our daughters.

I kept on with the tattooing, and in London I swam every morning in an open-air pool in the valley of a park in Brixton as police helicopters circled high above me in the warming air. I would swim for maybe an hour and then buy a short black coffee from a little beach hut and drink it as the morning sun rose, and the pool water lightened to a radiant blue that you might have said, if you thought about these things at all, was like the light of heaven you were always being told about when you were a kid.

I'd watch the sun come up and transform the pool and then I'd go to work with the picture of shining blue water in my head. I was still labouring and staying out late at night and it was not easy to swim every day, but it seemed important. I began to feel strong as my painted arms pulled me through the water every morning and I counted off the kilometres. On my days off I was there when the pool opened and I would stay until the late afternoon, when the sun began to fall behind the horse chestnut trees in the park. I'd sit on the decking with the last sun worshippers and Lido mums, the last stoners and old boys storing up the heat, the last young gangsters in low rider shorts and war tattoos waiting for the night. Together we would watch the setting sun make new patterns on the darkening water and on the last swimmers of the day.

People remember me, I guess because of the tattoos. One Saturday morning the top lifeguard, a blond, enormous South African named Bear, big as two men and with flip-flops thick and wide as swim floats, called to me as I was walking past his chair after a swim. His curly yellow hair was dark and tamped down with water.

"Hey, Tattoo Man," he said, "you all right?"

"I'm good mate thanks," I said.

"You got a minute to come up here? There's something I want to ask you."

Bear watched the water and did not look at me when he was speaking. He was wearing Arnettes but I knew Bear had blue eyes. I had noticed when we had spoken before that his left eye had a round gold cast in it. I climbed the ladder and from Bear's chair I could see clouds of pink dust raised by a group of young black men playing football in the rising heat on an unfenced gravel pitch in the park. There were a couple of older guys my age keeping up with the game. The game was fast and hard. I could taste the gritty dust the men raised and took into their mouths as they ran. I could see people walking dogs, people running, or making Tai Chi forms, or sitting under trees opening purple cans of lager. I could see the patterns people made on the day. What breeze there was gently moved the golden pool flags Bear had posted on the red brick walls and came softly to me. Bear reached back to shake hands.

"You ever think about being a lifeguard Kim?" Bear said with his back to me, "I'm running a course starting next week. Two week course and there's a job here at the end of it."

"Why me?"

"I need someone to help me with these kids I've got working here, and you look to me like you might be a water man."

That's how I started at Brixton Beach. I lived there, really, for the next few summers. I told myself I had everything I needed at the pool. In the winters Bear and I chased the summer and travelled all around. I'd read somewhere that the danger of civilisation is that you will piss your life away on things that don't matter, and that made sense to me.

May to October we opened the pool at six in the morning. I'd do my lengths first at about five while it was still dark. I guess you don't need me to tell you that the water's cold first thing in the morning but if you know what you're doing you can find what you need in cold water. After my swim I'd bring in the milk and bread and the breakfast pastries and get hot coffee made for the early morning swimmers. I'd sweep out and hose down the changing rooms and showers and check the pump room, made sure that was all ticking over, and that the chemicals were going into the water on a steady feed. I'd skim the pool for leaves and bugs and get my early shift guards cold water whenever they wanted it. Then I'd go sit up in the deep end chair, the same one Bear first talked to me from. The chair faced the sun as it rose in the morning. That's why I sat in it first thing. It was the best seat to get a tan on and it was either Bear or me sat in it in the mornings.

In the morning you'd be hard pushed to get people to believe there was anything to the job. You just sit in the sun and look at the girls and soak up the rays is what it must look like. All I can say is that you've got to know what you're doing and sitting up there eight or nine hours a day doesn't suit everybody, far from it. Me, I've been watching the water all my life. You might get thirty or forty people swimming in the morning but by noon on a hot day we would have over a thousand in with another few hundred locked outside and sweating in the park.

I'd work the mornings and later I'd go sit by myself by the pool and maybe sleep for a little bit and then be back on the pool for the late afternoon. We closed at seven. At about eight when Bear fired up the barbie and opened the bar I'd go shower in the big empty changing rooms and put on a clean pair of boardies and a Sun-Surf T-shirt. We had pool parties at night. Most days I'd work right through sixteen, seventeen hours lifeguarding and running the bar. We both knew better, but most often Bear would get something to keep us going, some MDMA powder maybe, some bliss, and we wouldn't sleep at all. Maybe we'd go night swimming with some girls. Get high round the pool and drink Iron Horse champagne under the stars. Don't let anybody tell you that you can't see the stars in London.

One morning a little kid about ten years old came into the pool on her own. She was mixed-race and curly haired and she wore a one-piece black Speedo under army greens. She had a hard but twinkly look on her face and she carried a brown, furry, smiling toy monkey that was a rucksack on her back. The monkey's long fringed arms that were the straps of the bag crossed in front of her like soft bandoliers and its big red-mouthed smiling face looked back at you as she walked past. She found a shaded place under the corrugated tin roof of the pool café and she put down the monkey bag and talked to it.

She took off her little flip-flops and the little peaked khaki army cap that she wore and that was puffy with curly hair and she went to swim and play in the shallow end. I heard her tell the monkey to look after her stuff and make sure nobody took it.

One morning she was sitting up by the deep end, talking to herself and looking sad with her feet in the water. I thought she might have lost something. She was wearing black nail varnish on her toes and fingers. The varnish had gone all crumbly, and she was picking at it and watching tiny flakes of black paint fall and float and be carried away on the pool water.

When I knelt down next to her so that she was in shadow she looked me up and down and said, "Why have you got all those tattoos? Don't you like yourself?"

A few days later I had the morning off and came in for a swim. It was a morning for swimming it felt like, warm and with little breezes riffling the surface of the water. Straightaway I felt light in the water and the water was soft and fast. I swam for a long time until the sick feeling I had gone into the water with was gone. Cold water and swimming are the only hangover cure I know that works. The girl was standing by the pool when I got out. She had her arms folded and she was looking at me like she'd never seen me before. The soft breeze lifted the curls of her hair that were becoming blonde in the sunshine. She had that sandy lion look all of our girls get on in the summer but I saw it on her first.

"Who'd have thought you'd be a good swimmer?" she said.

She came and sat by me when I was drinking overheated coffee and talking to a heavyweight Greek lifeguard called Nick at the shallow end. She had her monkey bag with her and she reached in and brought out rice cakes and a carton of mango juice and she ate her lunch and watched the water with me. She had her cap on and the cap was dark and wet from her hair. Nick and I sat in plastic chairs watching the pool, and Lee sat between us. She watched us looking straight ahead and talking without looking at each other.

"What's your name?" she said.

"I'm Kim and this is Nick. How about you?"_"Lee," she said, "I've got a boy's name and you've got a girl's name."

Nick laughed.

"What's the monkey's name?" I said.

"It's a bag stupid," she said, "It doesn't have a name. It's just a bag, see?"

She kind of waved the bag in front of my sight line.

She sat picking rice cake crumbs from her lap and looking at the water. She was quiet for a little while.

"I want to swim in the deep end but my Mum says I'm not allowed," she said.

"Kim'll take you," Nick said.

He was wearing a big sombrero with a pink patterned upturned brim and his black swim trunks and he was sitting back in his plastic chair so that only two legs of the chair were on the floor, his legs stretched right out so that his body was kind of arched up to the sun. It looked a hard way to sit and watch the pool but Nick was getting his tan on and, like always, he saw everything in the water that he needed to see.

"Sure," I said, looking over at Nick. "I'll take you. Do you think that'll be all right with your Mum?"

"My Mum's got a boyfriend," Lee said.

Nick laughed so hard coffee came out of his nose. Little kids went by in the water and our feet were splashed and cooled by the water they raised as they passed. A couple of the kids looked at Nick and laughed. He swung his chair down onto four legs and scooped water out of the pool and washed his face.

"You all right there Speedo Gonzales?" I said to Nick.

"Just trying to help you out Kim," Nick said, "I've seen her Mum."

Lee gave Nick a fierce little kid stare. Nick grinned whitely from the darkness of his face.

The next Sunday after church, and to check me out I guess, Araba walked into the shining brilliance of the pool at noon on flat, brown, beloved African feet that told me she would not be easily moved from any ground on which she chose to stand. She was swinging the beach bag she carried as though she were still hearing hymns, and she wore a summer dress and the secret smile she brings home from church. Lee stood between us looking from one of us to the other. She was wet from the pool and smiling at her Mum and me and kind of hopping about. I knew too, straightaway. A few days later when we were sitting in the park holding hands and watching Lee climb a tree, Araba said that she was pregnant with Jay, my adopted daughter. Just a year later we had Suzy.

When we started, and for a year or so afterwards, I used to tell Araba that the sun came up in the morning with her and she never wanted to hear it because words don't put food on the table, or take care of the babies, or look after the woman you say things like that to in any way that matters. Araba wants to know what you are going to do for the people you say you love. She wanted to know if I was going to stick.

If she heard me talking to you like this she'd tell me

to put in pictures of her when she was a little girl in the west country, sitting in meadows thick with rosemary. At school the kids held me down, she'd say, and at home sometimes I used to try and scrub the colour off me, but I remember too the banks of cowslips and wild garlic by the river, and fields of burnt grass to walk across in the rising heat of summer mornings. There were Bible stories, and my father playing the songs of Manuel de Falla on the guitar he'd learnt to play under the blood orange afternoon skies of Cape Coast when he was a boy.

Araba has taught me to be tough, not in the old ways, but tough enough to face down my ghosts and the voice inside that's always trying to do me harm. Araba's had plenty of fires and riots of her own. Araba does not want how I feel about her to be about her blackness, but still though, and I don't know how this sounds and can't say what it means, in the brownness of her skin is where I find again the transformed summer bodies of the girls of my home and boyhood. There's some connection there that I can hear humming between us, and though I don't know that she'd like to hear it, it's too late now not to tell the truth.

The first night we stayed together Araba, fierce, warm, unaccountable, royal, said: So what is with the tattoos? Her crucifix flashed in the dark. I said well it's a long story. I'm not going anywhere, she said.

WHEN I think about Scott in prison I always think about
my brother at night, when his hard mask was put away
with his too big prison shoes until he needed them again
in the morning. He is awake in the dark, locked down,
and tracking the noise of the prison that would wash
over you, I guess, as an aggregate of sound in the day
but in the lights out hours would be impossible not to
separate out and think about. It's never quiet in those
places, Neal told me once. There's a lot of screaming, he
said, especially at night, and it's at night, when you're
alone with yourself, that you have to bite down hard not
to add your voice to all that noise.

I have a small glass fronted bookcase at home like the
one Steve Tardelli had in his house when we were kids,
and in there I keep an old creased polaroid of Scott and
Neal wearing bright Ben Sherman shirts, sun washed
Levi's with a cuffed turn, and shined up twelve eye
boots and red braces. The picture was taken in front of a
bar they used to drink in sometimes called The Pier
Hotel. The bright sun is all on Scott. The wall they are
standing against is pocked in places and worn looking,
sandy Mediterranean pink and cut in half on a diagonal
by the shadow of another building. The shadow line cuts
across Neal and his head and left shoulder only are in
the sun. The top of the picture cuts off the name of the
bar painted in faded red paint on the wall so that the
picture seems be top edged in blood. I don't know why
the picture was taken or who took it, and I don't
remember how I came to have it. The picture might have
been taken anywhere hot and sun washed except for the
way Scott and Neal are dressed.

I could guess but I don't know why Scott drank in
The Pier Hotel. To get away from all the plotting and
aggro. It was known as a neutral ground bar you went
into if you were at the top of whatever game you were
playing. I think Dug drank in there from time to time
before he flipped out, and some of the high up Persians,

and tough, tough people you wouldn't even know lived in the town, but Scott warned me off going in there so I don't know. Donnie Orange worked on the door. You'd see his lemon Cresta parked up round the back. In the picture Scott and Neal have their arms around one another and they are not looking into the camera but into one another's eyes and they are smiling, smiling. It's hard to remember when we were so young. I guess they are drunk and high but I don't know and it doesn't matter. What you see and what draws you in are the bright true smiles of my brother and his good friend. And what does Scott feel when he thinks about Neal dead and ruined in the ground? I don't think about Scott enough, how he feels about things, and that's the truth.

One true thing I can say is that the only picture I have of Scott from that summer was taken outside a bar I never went into and by somebody I don't know, and my brother is smiling for reasons I don't understand, except to say why not smile, when you're young and high in the summer with your best friend? I just hardly ever saw him smile then is the thing. Maybe the truth is I just didn't make my brother smile much that summer, and so the picture tells me that although I maybe wanted to tell Scott's story I've only really told you mine, and Scott would tell you something different again.

A year or so ago, like I said, I met up with Scott in Morocco. There were some things I wanted to tell him but we argued, and when I left on the Casablanca bus in the morning sunshine with my girls, Scott was sitting on the beach wondering what he had done to me that I didn't love him anymore.

Last spring Scott surfaced in a place called Southmead, just outside Bristol. He hadn't lived in this country for fifteen years. In July, on my brother's birthday, I went across on a hot coach from Victoria to see him.

Scott pulled up outside the station in a Camper van. He was listening to a pumping Coco Tea and Luciano track called *Rough Inna Town*, and he was talking on the phone. He leaned over to let me in. "Basically," he was saying to whoever was on the other end of the phone, "It's been all downhill, bit of a cruise mate. Yeah that roundabout there, I suppose, it was heaving but so what, I'm just in and out man you know? Yes mate, I'm just picking him up now. All right, talk to you later."

Scott threw the phone onto the dash so that it hit with a hard plastic bash, and we hugged. We were both wearing shades, Arnettes, so I could not see his eyes and he could not see mine. Scott was tan and packed into himself like always. The red stubble on his head was coming in blond with splashes of grey. He was wearing a faded green vest, boardies and sandals.

"That was Zoyd," he said, "bloke I share with I told you about. Wants to know what time we're eating. He's visiting his kids and he wants to make sure he gets back in time."

"What we having?"

Scott pulled a joint out from somewhere.

"We're having this first," he said, "you still diving?"

I started diving like I did a lot of things, just to get the sight of Dug standing over me out of my head. Nothing gets to me down there, not Scott or Dug or the kid whose face I broke. I've got around some myself now. Mexico and Hawaii, Borneo and Ghana and the Southern Red Sea and a bunch of other places besides.

I've seen some things. I've swum at night with eagle rays off Black Rock, Maui, seeing the rays only because they flew above me showing their bone clean white undersides outstretched. The rays moved through the water like dreamed spaceships in black space, the gold lights of the Sheraton hotel shining on the surface of the water high above me and above the gliding rays like distant stars.

I've seen a man lying paralysed on the cold wet deck of his own boat go blind with a neurological bend off the coast of Jastania, in the Hel peninsular, Poland. The cold black Baltic Sea very deep, the man lying blind on the deck of his own boat had told us, very dark, very dangerous. The man that saved his life, Antonio lets call him, sweet Antonio, dead now.

I've swum through plankton thick and dark as falling soot, and fields of depthless never ending, never beginning violet blue water in the South China Sea. I've seen thousands of starfish in an Irish cave flaring off my fins like yellow leaves flying in October air. I've swum in a shale bottomed cave lit by the rainbow light of a quilt of pastel anemones on the cave's lee wall, the black exhaling forms of other divers almost sunlit in the clarity of the water in St. Kilda, far west of the Hebrides, over fifty metres down. Once, I found myself at the bottom of a cold black sea moving towards a lighted door that was only lighted, and only a door, in my head. When I dive I remember Scott saying that what he was looking for was out there, and when I'm below the waves out there is where I am.

"Yes mate," I said, "I'm still diving."

We smoked and got into the sounds and Scott drove and after a while he pulled up outside a detached house in a quiet street. "This is us," he said.

He bossed the van up so that two wheels were on the pavement outside the house. It was a hot day, and Scott parked up in the shade made by the heart shaped leaves of a linden tree.

We went into the house. I kicked off my flip-flops in the hall. There were pairs of sandals, walking boots and flip-flops piled up. There was an open cupboard to the left of the doorway into the kitchen and there were surfboards, boogie boards, waterproofs and Frisbees in there. There were a couple of old, worn rucksacks stacked up and bagged up hammocks. Later in the bathroom upstairs I saw Scott's weathered wash bag hanging from the wall, packed and ready to go.

Scott told me to go on through. The big front room was a knock through made of two smaller rooms. Above an open fireplace there was a map of the world in a plain frame. There was a large photograph of a white walled town in high mountains. "That's Zahara de la Sierras,"

Scott said, "I used to live there, Zoyd too. He was teaching English."

He pointed to a high house under open skies that would have had a sweeping view of the plains the mountain stood upon. "That was our house."

"What did you do out there?"

"Oh mate you know, the usual, nothing much. Knocking out some home grown and some bar work. Getting a tan on."

There was a blond fold-out wooden dining table by the window on the street side of the room, and at the left hand end there were French windows that opened out onto a long narrow garden. There was a concrete patio and some steps down to a small pond. There were kids toys on the grass and a clothesline with a couple of beach towels and board shorts on it.

My brother and I sat on fold-out camping chairs in the quiet garden in the warm sunshine. We drank the bottle of supermarket champagne I'd brought with me. Scott saw me looking at the new three-quarter sleeve of rocks, flowers and falling water on his right arm that covered up his old *Straight to Hell* tattoo.

"You not seen this?" he said.

"No mate. It's nice, where did you get that done?" I said, though I could tell.

"I went down to see your mate Steve back home. I've been meaning to go back and get the other sleeve done and cover up these." He had a couple of Death Heads on his left shoulder.

Zoyd came in around seven that night. He was a strong looking square blond man with dark eyes and a dry handshake and the same all purpose travelling accent that Scott had.

"It's good to know you mate," he said, "Scott talks about you all the time."

I looked over to Scott then but he'd left the room. Later Scott cooked and I went out for beer, and the three of us sat around and talked until late in the night. In the middle of a story Scott got up and went upstairs. Zoyd got me a fresh beer. I was halfway through it and Scott hadn't come down.

"Do you think I should check on him?" I said.

I went up and looked in on Scott. He was asleep on his bed and he looked about eight years old. I went down and told Zoyd.

"I think he's just happy to see you. He's been talking about you coming up for days."

Zoyd and I stayed up and we were talking and I was telling stories, I was drunk and high, and it came up that Scott had been in prison. Zoyd let the conversation go for a bit and then he said, "That's news to me. That Scott was in prison. I've known him for nearly fifteen years and he's never talked about it."

In the morning Scott drove to the beach at Weston. We were both a bit red eyed and I was feeling bad that I had said things to Zoyd that Scott would not have wanted me to say. We didn't talk about it of course. Scott's way when he felt rough was to not speak at all and pretend nothing had happened. As soon as we were in the van he lit up a joint. Things were the same they always were between us.

Scott let out a breath he seemed to have been holding for a long time, and said,"You think it's only you thinks about what happened. You go on about me being in prison to people you don't know. You ever think I might not want you to tell people about it? Look, when I left there I could carry prison around and let it ruin my life or do the things I always wanted to do. I'm a different person to the one you remember. Don't you want to know about some of the places I've been?"

At Weston Scott parked the van at the north end of the beach in a high part of town overlooking the sea and we walked back down the hill with the sea on our right, Scott walking ahead quickly but without effort as far as I could tell, wearing a worn green forage cap and carrying a small backpack. We sat on the beach.

I told Scott that I was ready to take responsibility for the things I did and the things that happened to me. I told him I was going to stop hiding behind him like I'd been doing all my life. Scott listened, and later, he told me stories about India.

"We should go out there together," he said, "You, me, Araba, the kids."

"Maybe we could one day Scott," I said, "We'd love that."

You would know, if you looked at us once, that we were brothers. How many times had we walked into the cold sea together? On the wet shining sand Scott searched me out with the Frisbee and when he found me and I caught it he smiled. In the afternoon as the sun began to fall we walked together back to the van, two dark forms against the sun, and it was like the walk home from the beach when we were boys even though I had never been to this place before and Scott was just passing through on his way back, he said, into Indonesia and then Japan. We walked the long sandy beach together in the golden light and with the sound of the sea all around.

AT PEVENSEY Bay I watch my children play on the beach.
They get their colour on in the summer, like their
mother, like me. Their skin fades and darkens with the
changing seasons of the year, and I see the habits of my
life reflected in their different shades.

Jay's never cut hair is braided and hanging past her
waist. She wears new boy's blue swimming trunks. Jay is
formal, correct, withheld with everybody except me and
her mother. She has started biting her fingers and I see
that the skin around her nails is red and sore. When she
was tiny we weren't sure about each other, or maybe I
was the one who wasn't sure and she read that in me. As
she's got older we've been kind of amazed about how
crazy we are about each other. Jay's never seen her real
Dad. He lives in another country but I wouldn't know
where. I don't think about it much, there isn't time.

When Jay's older I'll tell her some things I've learnt.
I'll tell her I never knew my Dad, and all my life I have
believed that he left Scott and Mum because of me,
because of my about-to-be. And that this has left a hole
in me that can't be filled, or so it seems, even after all
these years. I do know, because Lee sees her Dad, that
I'm the only person in our family who will know how
Jay feels when she starts to wonder what her real Dad is
like. So I'll tell Jay that I love her, and because I love her
and love being her Dad, I'll help her find him when it
comes to it like I know it will. I couldn't say I loved her
otherwise and expect her to believe me.

Suzy is burly and strong, and she has corkscrew
sandy lion's hair that's beginning to locks up. She's got a
fat little tummy that she likes to stroke and thick legs
and she's got my high insteps. She carries a perfect
dream world around in her head that the real world is
sometimes hard pushed to match, and how she feels is
dependent on how closely each moment of her life
measures up to her high expectations. For Suzy I know

that being by the sea is pretty close to being in that perfect world inside. It's her favourite place and I am happy I have been able to give that to her. It's in her blood, and not for the first time I wonder how my Dad could look at himself in the mirror, and then I remember that there have been plenty of times when I've found it more than difficult so who am I to say? Still I hate using that word about him, Dad, and wish there was another word for men who make you but who are never there.

"Lee's painted her hair black," Jay says, biting her fingers, "Mummy shouted at her and Lee-Lee told her to eff off."

"Lee's fourteen," Araba said, brushing Jay's hair out of her eyes, "that's what you do when you're fourteen."

"I won't tell you to eff off when I'm fourteen," Suzy said.

"Thank you baby," Araba said.

"Dad?"

"Dad?"

"Dadda!"

"Yes Jay, yes darling."

"What's your favourite animal between...a polar bear and an elephant?"

"That's a hard one Jay."

"I know Dadda."

"I like the word, elephant."

"Elephant, elephant, elephant."

"That's right Suzy."

"But you know I like polar bears."

"I know Dadda."

"If I had an elephant I'd take him swimming in the sea and I could sit on him and he could spray all the children with his trunk."

"You'd like that wouldn't you Suzy?"

"Yeah, it'd be fun."

"Dad?"

"Yes Jay."

"Isn't it that all polar bears are left handed?"

"Yes Jay."_

"You and me are left handed aren't we?"

"Yes Jay."_

"Yey! My Dadda!"

Araba and the kids swim and afterwards we eat the picnic my Mum and Araba have brought for us, flasks of coffee and cartons of hummus and pita bread and olives and juice and little treats, and after eating we all lay in the sun holding hands. Suzy falls asleep sucking her thumb. I cuddle Jay and watch Suzy sleeping like a dark cub, long lashed and peachy cheeked. I watch her with my heart. Awake, she's lit up by a blazing, questing intelligence that I recognise and love. She talks and talks, full to popping with the world. "Stop reading my mind," she'll say, or, "smell my head," but she's asleep now, and we are quiet. She huffs and flickers in her mother's lap and makes a noise like a bear cub. I sing one of Mum's favourites, '*Wake Up Little Suzy*,' that has become the song we all sing for her. Araba and Mum and Jay sing it with me. She's the baby and she plays on that but it's okay.

Jay's four and little Suzy is three. It's a simple enough thing. When I'm in the sun on the beach after swimming I'm home. That's as plain as I can put it. Everything is in place, an old familiar buzz in my heart and on my skin. It's something I want to give to the girls. I don't think that would be too bad. It might not seem so, but most of everything else I've done since the summer I've told you about has been to try and get that feeling back, to shore me up against everything else I'm often driven to feel and remember. Araba gives me that feeling all the time. Just by looking at me she warms me.

Later we go to my Mum's house. She lives close to the beach in an oyster cottage. Mum is not yet sixty. She is small and graceful and exact in her movements, still tan and tawny, still a beach girl. The hard years show in the lines of her face and the sadness in her eyes. I do not think that what Scott and I owe her can be paid back but it's up to us to try. She does not like my tattoos but she gets it that they work, that on some level they are part of

211

a story where her sons comes back to her at the end.

I have kept my back covered all day, and Mum and Araba and the kids haven't seen my new tattoo.

"Dad show us your new tattoo," Jay says.

"Yeah show us Daddy," Suzy says, "show us show us show us."

"There's still a lot to do," I say, "Steve reckons another twenty eight hours," and standing in my mother's beach garden under falling southern sunlight I take off my T-shirt and show them. The dried blood sticks and hurts when I take the shirt off.

Steve has put on the outline of a cloud chased, three masted schooner under full sail and close to land the full length of my back. The ship seems to jump and move on my skin. There are five English roses across my shoulders and two swallows flying in advance of the ship. Steve has lined out finger waves and little surf sprays. Below the ship there is a scrolled banner and a single word tattooed.

"There's a lot of blood Dad," Jay says.

"What's it say Dad," Suzy says.

"You can read Jay, tell your sister what it says."

I can feel Jay's hot breath on my back as she leans in close to read.

"Homeward," my daughter says.

Acknowledgments

Ponyboy, Sodapop, and Darry Curtis, Johnny Cade and Dallas Winston, are characters in S. E. Hinton's novel, *The Outsiders* (1967)

Thanks to Jim MacAirt, formerly owner of *Good Karma Tattooing* in Eastbourne and now working out of *Into You 2* in Brighton, for tattooing me for going on ten years and for talking about tattooing and Buddhism. References to the specific designs and amuletic power of sea tattoos come from these conversations and from 'Sailors 'N Tattoos' by George L 'Doc' Webb, in *Tattootime Number 3: Music & Sea Tattoos*, edited by Don Ed Hardy (Honolulu. Hardy Marks, 1988), and Don Ed Hardy's own *Sailor Jerry Collins: American Tattoo Master* (Honolulu. Hardy Marks, 1994). Maarten Hesselt van Dinter's *The World of Tattoo: An Illustrated History* (Amsterdam. KIT, 2005), and Takahiro 'Horitaka' and Katie Kitamura's *Bushido: Legacies of the Japanese Tattoo* (Atglen. Schiffer, 2001), were also fine resources when researching the protective, empowering, and good luck significance of tattoos and tattooing in all cultures.

If we are peaceful, if we are happy, we can smile, and everyone in our family, our entire society will benefit from our peace: this mantra on the wall of Steve Tardelli's tattoo shop is taken from Thich Nhat Hanh's *Being Peace* (California. Berkeley, 1987).

I am grateful to Adjoa Andoh, Kester Aspden, Jeremy Cole, Mark Cunnell, Andrew Franks, Bob Gannon, Erin Golding, Meg Jensen, Matthew Loukes, George Mouratidis, Lesley Preston, and Duncan White for reading sections of the novel in manuscript.

Marine Boy is a book about boys and men, mostly, but without my Mum Gillian and my wife Adjoa it would never have been written.

ESTRELLA DAMN a *Slim Gunter Novel*
MATTHEW LOUKES

Slim Gunter tries to help people. People like Estrella Woolf. Woolf has too much money, too few scruples and attracts trouble like a night-bus. When Slim investigates the theft of Estrella's Tibetan artefact he doesn't expect to get more out of it than enough money to pay the rent and settle the tab in the off-licence. What he actually gets is a case involving strong drugs, rats in hats, bad policemen, Maltese crooks, pornography, a trip to the seaside, and murder. Slim's sweetheart Lady, Big Eddie Scarborough and academic Barclay Lloyd join forces to find out what is really going on. But nobody's telling the truth and everyone has something to hide, including Slim.

"Slim Gunter is a fantastic creation. Loukes' voice is as laconic and disillusioned as you'd hope, but it's also painfully honest & painfully funny."

- Jeremy Sheldon